Jennifer Grey loves her job as a police-beat reporter for the *CHICAGO DAY*. But she also loves policer officer James Purcell. When he is arrested for drug trafficking, Jennifer is shocked. Has Jim betrayed her and their growing love, or is there something going on here much deeper than anybody anticipated? The only man who can answer that question has been mortally wounded while making an arrest.

HEARTBEAT

Jerry B. Jenkins, is the author of more than fifty books, including the popular Margo Mystery Series, co-author of the best-selling *OUT OF THE BLUE* with Orel Hershiser, and *HEDGES*. Jenkins lives with his wife Dianna, and three sons at Three-Son Acres, Zion, Illinois.

Jerry B. Jenkins

HEARTBEAT

Book One In The Jennifer Grey Mystery Series

Flip over for another great
Jennifer Grey Mystery!
THREE DAYS IN WINTER

BARBOUR BOOKS
Westwood, New Jersey

One

At 12:53 A.M., Tuesday, December 6, Jennifer Grey awoke to the sound of the telephone beside her bed. "I know you don't want me to call you unless it's important, but I think this is hot." It was the voice of Robert Block, her young assistant at the *Chicago Day*.

"That's all right, Bobby," she said. "What've you got?"

"Another big internal bust. Lots of top names from the Sixteenth Precinct, but somebody went down tonight."

"Someone was shot?"

"Yup, don't know who yet. Rumor is someone from Internal Affairs."

"Killed?"

"Think so, but nobody's talking."

"Where are you?"

"The office. Leo told me you'd want to handle this yourself and to just stay by the phone."

"He's right."

"I could handle it for you, Jennifer, if you wanted me to, I mean."

Jennifer smiled at his earnest naiveté. "I'll call you from the Sixteenth, Bobby. But thanks anyway."

Jennifer spent less than two minutes washing her face and applying light makeup. She pulled her long, light-brown hair into a ponytail and threw on what she always thought of as her emergency outfit—a white, button-down blouse under a burnt-orange V-neck sweater, a brown plaid, pleated skirt, and zippered boots.

She grabbed her calf-length camel hair coat and slung over her shoulder a large bag containing the usual essentials plus her reporter's spiral note pad.

She paused near the phone in the living room, wondering if this was the one time she could justify taking advantage of her relationship with Jim. She had enjoyed a lovely dinner with him just hours before at a quiet spot not frequented by newspaper people or policemen.

She knew it was risky, if not wrong, for a police reporter to be seeing a policeman. But she rationalized that if she didn't use him as a source of information and left writing about him to the feature writers—his current assignment took him into elementary and junior high schools as Officer Friendly—no one had to know.

Besides, she wasn't sure how she felt about him. It was clear how he felt about her. But a widow of fewer than three years who still thought of her late husband every day was not jumping into any new relationship.

There was no need to bother Jim in the middle of the night. Chiding herself for having even thought of waking him, she sat on the edge of the sofa and dialed the Sixteenth Precinct station instead.

"Yeah, somethin' went down, honey," Desk Officer Flannigan told Jennifer. "But if I tell ya over the phone, that means I won't get to see yer pretty face down here tonight, right?"

"Please, Herb," she said, "you can't joke about someone getting killed, can you?"

Silence.

"Herb?"

"Who bought it, Jenny? I didn't know anybody bought it. I heard a guy took a coupla slugs in the gut, but I didn't know he died."

"Who was it, Herb?"

"Somebody from IAD, but you know I can't tell you anything. You sure he died? I didn't hear he died."

"My source wasn't sure either, Herb. I just thought you might know."

"You don't know any more'n I do. What're you doin' talking about somebody dyin' when you don't know?"

"I'm sorry, all right? Can I talk to Campbell? Is he on tonight?"

"He's on, but he's talkin' to nobody, 'specially the press. And I'm not supposed to either. You understand?"

"If I come down there, can I see him?"

"I doubt it, but then I'd get to see you, so don't let me talk you out of it."

Jennifer might have appreciated the tacky compliment under other circumstances. But she had been poking around the grimy precinct station houses for almost a year since graduating from obituaries and school board meetings, and she had no inkling of more Internal Affairs Division activity right under her nose. A major operation had taken place with her on the beat every day, yet she knew nothing about it.

Worse yet, someone from Internal Affairs was probably fighting for his life. A new widow might be in the making, and she felt that pain again.

She phoned downtown headquarters, but she got no new leads. *Jim will understand,* she decided. But the phone at his apartment just rang and rang.

Shortly after midnight, a task force for the Internal Affairs Division of the Chicago Police Department had scheduled the operation that would rock the department to its core.

Yet another contingent of Chicago's finest had been caught wallowing in its own mire. Not yet a year and a half since the biggest internal scandal in its history had seen dozens of police officers sentenced to prison for trafficking in dope, another black eye on the police department's reputation was swelling.

No one—least of all the guilty officer—knew of the investigation. Most officials and citizens and even the press assumed that the last housecleaning had scoured the department of the worst offenders and probably scared the small-timers into staying straight.

But a tiny, close-knit unit from IAD had been keeping an eye on suspicious activity in the Sixteenth Precinct for nearly thirty months—in fact, since long before the more publicized crackdown had even been initiated.

This band of four were players in one of the most dangerous games in the world. Not even their families could know of their activities. They had been given routine assignments, many requiring uniforms, while in actuality they were undercover agents, spying and ratting on their own colleagues.

There can be no more despised good guy than the one who must make his living deceiving his friends, being a snitch, a stool pigeon. It took a special kind of person to even be considered for such an assignment, and only those a cut above the rest lasted a year.

When you were suspected of reporting to Internal Affairs, you were shunned even by your friends, even by good cops who had nothing to hide. You were quietly ridiculed for being a goody-two-shoes, an idealist, a superpatriot, a God-squadder. And soon enough, of course, you had to be reassigned. A known employee of Internal Affairs was worthless.

Thus, the noisy crackdown that resulted in arrests and convictions and sentences for so many Chicago cops made the smallest IAD unit fear for the success of their own surveillance of the Sixteenth Precinct.

Would their activities be revealed in the course of the trial? Would success of the bigger mission scare off their prey before they could lower the net? No one from the special unit had been involved in the major crackdown, but would all the publicity somehow tip their hands?

Would Jennifer Grey, the woman they begrudgingly admired for always being in the right place at the right time, somehow sniff out this terribly delicate operation? Could she or the *Day* be persuaded that their First

Amendment rights should be voluntarily limited for the sake of human lives?

For months after the publicity of the previous noisy crackdown, IAD laid low, finally realizing that their mission had not been aborted. Their targets had become more cautious, but the lure of profit had finally brought them scurrying back into the cesspool.

And the men from IAD, the ones who had avoided suspicion and had been able to rise above the feeling that they were betraying their comrades, if dope-dealing policemen could be considered comrades, were waiting.

They waited for the perfect time. They waited for the perfect opportunity. They waited until they had something solid on each of the three men and one woman they had been tailing.

The midnight roundup was to be a simple maneuver. At a meeting earlier in the day, the four IAD officers had mapped careful strategy, plotting the whereabouts of their marks. Lieutenant Frank Akeley would be easy. He'd leave his favorite watering hole on Wells Street at exactly midnight, and IAD Chief John Lucas and two specially assigned patrolmen—who would not know what they were going to be involved in until about half an hour in advance—would make the arrest, booking Akeley downtown in an attempt to avoid publicity as long as possible.

The two others would be trickier. Sergeant Bill Much was a family man and would be asleep at home, if everything went as expected. No one looked forward to the prospect of an arrest in the dead of night, especially when a man's family would suddenly realize what was going on.

They'd think it was a mistake, of course, but Sergeant Much would know. And he could be armed. And there could be trouble. IAD Special Investigator Ray Bequette had the assignment, and he also would take two uniformed police offficers with him.

For Officer James Purcell, IAD had decided on a ruse. He was a bachelor, living alone in an apartment on Oak Street near Rush. IAD investigator Donald Reston, a rangy, athletic, youthful man in his late thirties, would call Purcell from the lobby and tell him he had information on one of his cases. Reston would say he was sorry to bother him, but could they come up, and all the rest. When Purcell activated the buzzer and let them in downstairs, they could only hope he would still be unaware of what they were up to.

At least the bust that would end Reston's stint in IAD (anything publicized ruined future effectiveness) would be one the public would love. They turn on their heroes the first chance they get, and Purcell was a bona fide turncoat against the public trust.

Any bad cop was, of course, but this one would go down the throat of John Q. Public like nectar. A bad cop with a good reputation who gets his comeuppance. For Reston, it was too good to be true.

Officer Trudy Janus would be on duty on the street. Her partner would be directed to phone the station for a personal message. When he stopped to place the call, IAD's Eric O'Neill, a uniformed officer, and a police matron would arrest Janus.

It was set. Warrants had been issued. And not more than eight people in the world knew what would be going down. Fewer than that knew when and who and how. The mayor and the police commissioner knew the basics. IAD Chief Lucas, the three others in the operation, and a secretary knew everything.

Lucas was convinced that his men had not breathed a word to anyone, not anyone. Not a friend, not a relative, not a lover. If ever there was a business in which you couldn't trust anyone, this was it. Not that a man like Ray Bequette couldn't trust his wife of twenty years, but who might she tell? What might slip? Who knew what information might get to the wrong ears?

That was one reason that short terms with IAD were the norm. A man couldn't carry the burden of guilt and suspicion long without being able to tell even his own loved ones.

The operation was to be simultaneous, with the four suspects being brought downtown by 12:30 A.M. Sergeant Bill Much would be last, as his arrest would take place on the city's far West Side. Many more officers and civilians were involved, of course, but one thing was sure: these four were the ringleaders, the principal drug buyers and suppliers. And when they fell, they'd bring a massive network down with them.

At 11:00 P.M. IAD Chief John Lucas had sat in his personal car on the other side of the street and a half block to the south of the tiny parking lot of The Illusion bar near the corner of Wells and Ontario. Unmarked squad cars would never work for Internal Affairs; they were just as recognizable by cops as were the standard blue and white patrols.

Lucas, a tall, thin, graying man in his late fifties, was as respected as a man in his position could be. His was a thankless job. Neither he nor the people above him ever really liked what he ferreted out. Yet no one, not even those who had been burned by his professional approach and his incredible reputation for confidentiality in a huge police department, questioned his motives.

He was always impeccably dressed and soft-spoken. He shunned publicity. He personally handled the arrests of police officers above the rank of sergeant, and as difficult as it must have been for him, he was somehow usually able to pull them off with the least humiliation for the suspect.

That, he told his superiors more than once, would come in greater measure than he could ever personally mete out, when the man had to face his own family and the press and the public in court. "It is not my job to destroy a man before his subordinates. By the time I get to him, he has already accomplished that on his own. My role is to clean house quickly and deliver the man to his fate."

His prey had entered the bar, as usual, a few minutes after ten-thirty. While Lucas's men began to close their stakeout nets around Sergeant Bill Much's West Side bungalow and Officer James Purcell's Near North apartment and Trudy Janus's squad car, Lucas himself unhurriedly left his car and strode to a phone booth on the corner, another half block north.

He could still keep an eye on the bar's side exit—the one Lieutenant Frank Akeley would use to get to his car. Lucas and his men had talked about having a squad car merely pull Akeley over with a story of a burned out taillight or some other minor infraction. Then, when his guard was down, he would be arrested and read his rights.

But Lucas had decided against it. Too dangerous, he believed. Akeley was usually able to pilot himself to his apartment, despite the fact of driving while under the influence. But Lucas didn't know specifically what kind of a drunk Frank Akeley made. He was armed. Would he cry or pass out, or would he reach for his piece? It was too great a risk for the patrolman or two who would have no idea what it was all about until it was over.

Lucas dialed. "Sixteenth Precinct, Flannigan."

"Good evening, Officer Flannigan," Lucas began carefully. "Chief Lucas calling for the sergeant on duty."

"Yeah, who's 'is again?"

"Chief Lucas calling."

"An' you want Sergeant Campbell?"

"If he's the sergeant on duty, yes sir."

"Is this Lucas from IAD?"

"Yes, sir."

"What's goin' down? Somethin' big?"

"Flannigan," Lucas grew cold. "I need to speak with your watch commander. Will you put him on please?"

Lucas directed Campbell to assign two patrolmen to meet him at the phone booth as soon as possible. "Oh, please, Chief, you're not gonna bust somebody right here on my shift, are ya?" Campbell pleaded.

"As a matter of fact, no, Sergeant, and you know I can't discuss it further. May I expect a couple of officers?"

"Yes, sir."

Lucas turned his collar up against the cold wind and buried his hands deep in the pockets of his long trench coat. When a squad car pulled to the curb, he slipped into the backseat and briefed the officers.

They began by radioing in that they would be unavailable for more than an hour. Lucas told them precisely what he was doing and—not so precisely—why. "You will station yourself in front of the bar, out of the light," he told the one, "and you will be in front of the next building to the north. When I leave my car and cross the street, I will approach Lieutenant Akeley and call him by name, as if in a greeting.

"If he merely looks up in surprise, just fall in behind me in the parking lot to back me up. I'll identify myself officially, show him my badge, and ask him to surrender his weapon. If he resists, I'll ask you to assist me. Don't draw your guns unless I ask you to or unless it becomes obviously necessary."

The officers, one young and the other old, were stony. Neither liked his assignment, but Lucas didn't detect any treason in their silence. He didn't much like his own assignment for that matter. Nonetheless, this wasn't the time for convincing the patrolmen of the lieutenant's guilt. They wouldn't attempt to tip anyone off by radio, because they knew he would be monitoring the frequency in his own car.

"Take your positions at eleven fifty-five, unless you see me leave my car earlier."

Lucas headed back to his own car and maintained his vigil, shaking his head slightly at the thought of the watch commander worrying that one of his own men might be used by IAD. *What will he think when he finds out it's his boss, the lieutenant who likes to work the three to eleven shift, but always leaves for The Illusion at ten-thirty?*

On the West Side, Ray Bequette had rolled to a stop about a block from Bill Much's home. The only light visible in the house was a flickering television from an upstairs window. Bequette had briefed his assigned officers on the way from downtown. One moved quietly between houses to cover the back door; the other carefully hid in the shrubbery at the front of the small house.

"I'll ring the bell, and we'll just have to see what he does," the stocky forty-five-year-old veteran whispered. He had aspired to a position with IAD since its inception when he was a young cop. When he secretly supplied information leading to the arrest of not only three men on his shift, but also his own partner, in a shakedown scheme, IAD was able to keep his name out of it and put him on other cases while providing another assignment as the perfect front. He was ostensibly in charge of records and vehicles at the smallest precinct in the city. There was no way to keep his name out of this one. When he personally arrested a sergeant, the word would spread quickly and his undercover days in IAD would end.

At the Oak Street apartment of Officer James Purcell, Donald Reston had worried that Purcell would smell a rat. So when Purcell sounded not the least bit perturbed at being awakened by a phone call from the lobby and quickly agreed to let Reston and two others come up to see him, Reston sent one cop to one end of the hall and the other one to the other end and approached Purcell's door carefully.

Eric O'Neill had arranged for an emergency personal call to be placed to the precinct station for the partner of Officer Trudy Janus. When the dispatcher related the message, "Ten-twenty-one the station, personal," Janus's partner stopped at the next call box. As he neared the phone, the uniformed officer approached to tell him what was happening, while O'Neill and the matron closed in on the unsuspecting woman in the squad car.

Two

Officer Trudy Janus's partner had been puzzled when he was interrupted before reaching for the call-box phone. "There's no call," Eric O'Neill's backup told him. "IAD just needed you out of the car for a minute." He wheeled around to see O'Neill flash his badge through the passenger side window of the squad car while the matron positioned herself near the taillight on the other side.

Janus angrily yanked at the door handle, but O'Neill pressed against the door, both palms facing her. "You can step out," he said, "but I want to see those hands."

"What're you, bustin' me?" she asked.

"You got it. Lemme see those hands."

"I'm not goin' for the gun," she said, disgusted and swearing. "Hey, you can't collar me without a woman here anyway!" O'Neill pointed to the matron. When Janus craned her neck to look, O'Neill opened the door and asked her to unsnap her holster.

"Was my partner in on this setup?" she demanded.

"No."

"What's this all about?"

"You wanna just come downtown with me and find out, Trudy, or you want me to read you your rights right here while a crowd gathers?"

She stepped from the car and slammed the door.

"Should I have her search you, or you wanna give me your other piece?"

Janus pulled a tiny .22 from her left ankle.

"Is that everything?"

She nodded, glaring.

James Purcell had opened his apartment door to find Donald Reston out of his direct line of sight in the hall with his snub-nosed .38 in his hand. "Whoa! I'm unarmed, Don," Purcell said, barefoot in pajama bottoms and a T-shirt. "Search me."

"I'm on a job from IAD," Reston told him, almost apologetically, and holstered his pistol. He signaled his backups, and they entered the apartment.

"What's it all about, Don?" Purcell asked.

"It's about dope," Reston said. "Isn't it usually about dope?"

"Not always," Purcell said.

Reston squinted at him, wondering what he meant. "You wanna just come with us, or do you need me to officially arrest you here?"

"Nah. I'll come." Purcell didn't even appear offended.

When Ray Bequette had rung the front doorbell at the Bill Much residence, a huge figure appeared at the window upstairs. Ray waved, and Much opened the window. "Who'sat? Bequette? What're you doin' here, Ray?"

"I'm here for IAD, Bill. I'm sorry."

Much was bending over with both hands on the windowsill, his massive body still. He stared down at Bequette, a man he'd never worked with, but who had been a classmate at recruit school more than twenty years before.

Much's shoulders heaved and he began to sob. "Do I gotta come with you right now?" he whined.

"Yeah," Bequette whispered.

"Oh, no." Still Much didn't move except to draw a hand to his mouth and muffle his whimpering. "Oh, no, no." And he swore.

"C'mon down, Bill," Bequette said. "Just come on downtown with us, huh?"

"You're not alone?" the big man said.

"I got somebody at the back and somebody here with me," Ray said, and his front yard man extricated himself self-consciously from the bushes.

"Oh, you didn't have to do that, Ray. You know me. I ain't gonna hurt nobody. I'll come with ya. Just give me a minute."

"Bill?"

"Yeah."

"You come without your piece, hear?"

"'Course, Ray. I don't wanna hurt nobody." Lights began to come on in other rooms.

When Sergeant Bill Much, who would never wear a badge again, emerged from his house, he wore bedroom slippers, no socks, work pants with an elastic waistband, a sweatshirt, and a short, unbuttoned jacket. He carried a paper bag with a change of clothes. And no gun.

"Am I gonna be gone long?" he asked Bequette.

"Probably so."

"My wife can bring my other stuff in the morning," he said absently. He sat in the front seat next to Bequette, carefully placed the bag next to him, pressed his fingers to his forehead, and cried quietly all the way downtown.

When Bequette drove through the underground garage to the elevator that would take Much to the interrogation room, he saw Reston's and O'Neill's cars. John Lucas had not arrived yet, so Bequette, as special investigator, had to officially arrest and charge Much, Purcell, and Janus and see that they were properly booked.

Janus sat in a straight-backed wooden chair, coolly answering O'Neill's questions. She looked up in disgust at Bill Much's red, puffy eyes. Jim Purcell leaned against a counter, chatting amiably with a booking clerk.

He jerked quickly to attention with a stricken look when the rumor reached the booking room that "Lucas is down! They've taken him to Henrotin Hospital!" Much grimaced. Janus suppressed a smile.

John Lucas's backup officers had moved into position at 11:55 P.M. as instructed, and Lieutenant Frank Akeley left the bar six minutes later. He may have been tipsy, but it didn't show in his walk. He was in plainclothes, moving briskly between vehicles to his own car.

Lucas's path intersected Akeley's line of vision, but the lieutenant apparently decided not to turn and look, despite the fact that he had to have seen Lucas peripherally.

"Frank!" Lucas called, yet still the man didn't slow or turn.

By continuing, Lucas would have blocked Akeley, but he hesitated, then stepped forward again, falling in behind Akeley. "Frank!" he tried again, knowing full well that even an inebriated man would have heard him.

Akeley stopped, but he didn't turn around. Lucas signaled for his backups and put his hand on Akeley's shoulder. "What *do* you want, Lucas?" Akeley shouted, his back still to him.

"You know what I want, Frank. Don't make it difficult for both of us." He was glad Akeley's hands were in his overcoat pockets and that the coat was buttoned. He couldn't go for his shoulder holster without unbuttoning his coat.

But as Akeley turned around, the hand hidden by his body pulled a .22 from his coat pocket, and he fired three times as he faced Lucas. The IAD chief lurched forward, his face ashen, and he grabbed Akeley's lapels, dragging him to the ground before releasing his grip. Lucas was unconscious, bleeding from two holes in his abdomen and one hole in his chest.

"Police! Freeze!" the uniformed officers screamed as they dropped to crouching positions, each with both hands on service revolvers pointed at Akeley's head.

"Self-defense, self-defense! Lucas tried to kill me!" He still had the weapon in his hand.

"Drop it, or you're dead!"

"I'm your superior!" Akeley said, trying to pull himself up from under Lucas's weight.

"The man never made a move on you, Lieutenant!" the officer said, pulling back the hammer of the .38 with his thumb. Akeley let the .22 slip from his fingers and slumped again to the pavement as the other cop kicked it away.

"You probably killed the man," the first said. "We gotta call an ambulance."

Jennifer Grey tried to watch her speed as she hurried to the Sixteenth Precinct station house. She remembered the warning of Leo Stanton, her city editor, that he would bail her out of jail for whatever it took for her to get a story except a traffic ticket.

His idea of police reporting and hers were light years apart. But he was the one with thirty-five years in the business who had been on the police beat "when cops were cops and newspapers were newspapers."

With Leo Stanton in the slot, the *Chicago Day* would always have an old-fashioned, high quality, complete city news section, "even if," he was fond of saying, "the rest of the rag goes to psycho-babble, pinko columnists, and how to develop a meaningful relationship with your dog."

She enjoyed working for Leo, even if she couldn't stand the unlit cigar lodged in the corner of his mouth. Occasionally he'd slide it free with two fingers and a thumb and she'd have to endure looking at the soggy end, but he was a bit more articulate when his plug was pulled.

He'd had the crazy thing in the first night when she turned in a story he didn't like. She was new on the police beat and had written what he called "a feminine piece."

"But I'm a woman," she had tried. "I'm going to sound more like a woman than a man. I can't change that can I?" He glared at her. "Should I?"

"You should sound like a newspaper reporter, not a man *or* a woman. People don't want to read *you*. They want to read your story. Write it like a reporter, not like a pretty little lady."

He shoved her story back across the desk, and she couldn't resist yanking it from his grip. She knew she shouldn't have, but she was fuming, talking to herself. She headed back to her typewriter, but he called her back.

"This time," he said, "remember that you're in the city room now, not the society page or wherever in the world we inherited you from. Write it on the tube and patch it over to mine. I'll edit it on the screen."

It had taken her until midnight to learn the rudiments of the video display terminal so she could rewrite the story. Robert Block, a journalism intern from Northwestern University who was to be her assistant, walked her through it and even showed her how to transmit her story to Leo when she was ready.

Twice she had lost everything but her notes, but finally the piece was finished. She sent it electronically to Leo's machine. When it came up on the screen, he hollered across the city room, "This better be good; I'm two hours into overtime now, and everybody knows I don't get paid overtime."

She was still mad. *Everybody's seen your salary posted with all the other Guild rates too, she thought, and if we made that kind of money, we wouldn't care about overtime.* And as she sat waiting for his reaction, she realized how good it was to feel some real emotion again after so long.

After Scott had been killed in an auto accident just before their first anniversary, Jennifer had retreated to her parents' home in Rockford. She wanted to do nothing, to say nothing, to think nothing. When the shock wore off and the pain invaded, she slept twelve to sixteen hours at a stretch and didn't want to eat.

Her parents had been supportive, but her father brought her back to reality with his gentle speculation that her sleep was just a substitute for what she really wanted. She wanted to die, he said. She wanted to join Scott. She knew in an instant that he was right. And that she couldn't. And that the same God she had trusted as a child and had worshiped and prayed to all her life would bring her through this.

She knew it in her head, but that didn't make her feel any better. Though her father's counsel forced her back into a semblance of normal routine, the numbness, the absence of any emotion, hung with her like a colorless cloud even after she had moved away from home again. She found her own apartment and finished the last few hours of her journalism degree. Then she landed a job on the new *Day*, mostly because they wanted an entire staff that had not worked on a Chicago paper before.

She wrote obituaries and then covered board meetings, and her no-nonsense reporting style caught Leo's eye. Whenever he got on her case about anything, she reminded herself that *he* had sought *her* out, not the other way around. He was the one who thought she had the makings of an excellent police reporter. He was the one who said she could go places and that there was no better starting place than the toughest beat in the city.

"You'll be up against the best the *Tribune* and the *Times* have to offer," he said. "And they won't give you a thing."

On that first night, her anger at her new boss made her realize that she was emerging again. After a couple of years in emotional limbo, the temper that had so tried her mother, the temper she had even hidden from her young husband, the temper she had tentatively and unsuccessfully tried to turn on God when He snatched her love away came bubbling up to make her feel alive again.

Everyone knew what it was like to work for Leo. And everyone wanted to. You'd never learn so much so fast or be pushed to such limits or set such standards for yourself working for anyone else. But that didn't lessen her ire any when he read her rewrite and yelled at her again.

She stood at the rim of his horseshoe desk and heard him say one word she didn't understand. Was it good? *Bad? Better? Worse?*

"I'm sorry?" she said.

He repeated it, only this time it sounded like a foul expletive. It wasn't that she hadn't ever heard the word before; she just wasn't sure she'd heard it this time.

"I didn't hear you," she said.

He pulled his cigar from his lips, as if to aid his articulation, then thought better of it and waved her back to her desk. When she arrived, her screen was blinking. She called up the message and blinked herself. There on the screen, from her new boss, was the four-letter word she thought she'd heard.

She didn't want Leo to see her redden, more from anger than embarrassment. She tapped out a return message. "Does that mean you like my story, or you don't?"

"I don't," came the reply.

"Can you tell me why, or is vulgarity all I get?"

"There's no more time to mess with it. I'll rewrite it."

"Then you take the byline in the morning paper."

"The city editor take a byline on the front page? It's your stuff, your work. Anyway, I'm in charge of who gets bylines."

"It feels ridiculous writing you messages from twenty-five feet away. Just know that I'm going to succeed in this job and make you like me; appreciate me, anyway."

"*It* doesn't feel ridiculous. *You* do. So do I. And my liking you is of little consequence to the job we're paid to do. Appreciate you? I already do. Now go home, and in the morning, enjoy the story under your name. It'll be good."

And it had been good. Leo was a pro. The best. Earthy, but a mentor, nonetheless. They had not communicated, except face to face, since that first night. In fact, he had apologized for his language.

"I didn't know you were religious," he explained.

"I wouldn't call myself religious," she had said. "We can talk about it sometime."

"No, we can't. And I'm glad you don't call yourself religious, because religion doesn't go far on the police beat. You'll see."

A pro, a good mentor and all, but not always right. Jennifer had seen how the police beat and her faith jibed or didn't jibe all right, and she had to wonder how she would have survived without it.

She prayed now as she parked on the street across from the Sixteenth Precinct. She prayed for the injured cop, whoever he was. For his wife. For his family. For the people who would be hurt by this latest internal crackdown, whatever it was all about. For the people who had been hurt by unscrupulous cops in the first place, because there were always civilian victims when policemen went bad.

As she trotted across the street and up the steps to face the greasy Flannigan, she prayed for her Jim. He hadn't been pressed into late duty for months. She knew he wasn't scheduled for tonight.

But if the internal affairs arrests were significant or widespread, maybe a lot of the guys in the Sixteenth would be on the street.

Three

James Purcell had been one of the first men Jennifer had met in her new role with the *Day*. He'd been a detective in the Vice Control Division who had requested a transfer due to his personal scruples.

Much had been made of it in the papers because scruples hadn't been a problem in the Chicago Police Department for as long as anyone could remember. "I don't want to come off like a Sunday school type," the *Sun-Times* had quoted him. "But there are things a VCD detective has to do that make it hard for me to sleep at night. I want to see vice controlled in Chicago, but it takes a different kind of a man to do this job."

The public had taken him to its heart. What he really wanted, he said, was an assignment in the Homicide Division. There was a "Jim Purcell Day" and even a fan club. But it all blew over shortly after the police commissioner announced that it was not up to an individual officer to choose his assignment. The commissioner said he and his command officers would decide whether a man could beg off an assignment, and that even if they decided that such requests might be tolerated, there would be no selecting of the new assignment.

The implications were clear. An officer might request a transfer, but it would not have to be honored, and there was no guarantee he wouldn't be sentenced to some Siberia within the department, like the night desk clerk's job in the Sixteenth Precinct. Which is what Purcell received.

When Jennifer was making the rounds that first week, she found herself coming back again and again to the shy, younger-than-his-years-looking bachelor at the Sixteenth. She hadn't even entertained a thought of interest in him or any man, but she was scrambling in her job and she needed help. Other desk officer types on her beat leered at her. The brass tolerated her but hardly talked to her. Some tested her. Some made passes at her. Many treated her as a child.

She wanted to do a good job. She wasn't there to do public relations work for the police department, but she wasn't out to get anybody either. All she wanted was information. Solid, truthful, no games, complete information she could use to write a story the public had the right to hear.

Jim Purcell seemed to understand that when no one else did. And though he had said he didn't want to be considered a Sunday school type, he *was* a Sunday school type, and the kids he taught on Sunday mornings demanded an explanation after that quote appeared.

He was like an oasis. She could count on a smile from him even when she stopped at the station house in the middle of the night. She knew that at the end of the counter in front of his desk, she'd find a little wire basket full of copies of all the reports of arrests in the precinct since she'd dropped in last.

Her predecessor had told her about the wire baskets that were unpublicized sources of information to the press and the public. No one used them but the police reporters, and they were not to take the sheets or make photocopies. The desk officers in many station houses thought it cute to "misplace" all but the stray dog or cat-up-a-tree reports or, worse, drop in bogus reports.

Jim had rescued her from that humiliation as well. She showed up one night, took her usual copious notes based on the reports in the basket, heard once again that the watch commander didn't have time to talk to her about any of them, and proceeded to tell Jim of a report she had read in the last station house.

Jim's eyes grew wide with mock wonder as she recounted the story of a young mother who had reportedly been startled by an intruder. "But she just took the matters into her own hands. She shushed him with a finger to her lips as she rocked the baby, giving the intruder a look that said he'd better not wake the baby, whatever he did. Then she continued singing lullabies to the baby while the man sat on the floor. Within a few minutes, he was sound asleep, and she called the police. They got there just as he was waking up and—Jim! I've been had, haven't I?"

"Just one question," Jim said. "Did the watch commander talk with you about the report?"

"Yes."

"Has he ever talked to you about a case before?"

"No."

"Yeah. I'd say you've been had."

Jennifer turned it into points with her boss though, and she even turned the joke around on the men who started it. She wrote the story as if it were fact, until she got to the bottom line where she quoted herself, "And any reporter who'd buy this has to also believe in the Easter Bunny."

Leo got a good laugh out of it and told her he was glad she saw through it. She wanted to tell him that her new friend at the Sixteenth was really responsible for saving her from it. But Leo had warned her enough about not fraternizing that she thought better of it.

Then she got a buddy from the composition room to doll the story up in type as it might appear in the paper, had it laminated, and presented it to the desk officer. It quoted both him and his boss, and the look on his face when he thought it would be in the next day's paper was worth the embarrassment she had suffered in believing it in the first place.

When Jim Purcell was reassigned, after just a couple of months, to the role of Officer Friendly, it might have meant the end of their contact had it not been for Jennifer's independence. She remembered being disappointed the night he told her that he would no longer be on the desk after the end of the month, but still she felt no stirrings. He was just a nice guy, a rare Christian among a rough bunch of men. They knew little about each other, and neither was really supposed to fraternize with the other though this was only traditional on both sides, not written policy.

Then the night she had car trouble right in front of the station house, she was tempted to run back in and ask his help. But that would have been unprofessional. It might have even looked forward.

But she didn't have time to wait for a tow truck, and who knew what gas station would send one this time of night anyway? Should she call Bobby and have him come and get her? Who needed the heat that would bring from Leo? Leo didn't care if you were a man or a woman, he always said, "You've got your job to do and your deadlines to meet and you do it, that's all."

So she had called a cab, but she didn't use the pay phone in the precinct. She used a phone down the block where she waited for the cab until just after 11:00 P.M. But the car that finally pulled to the curb was not a cab. A man, alone, rolled down the passenger side window. She started back toward the station.

"Hey! It's me, Jim! You need a ride?"

She felt foolish. "No, thanks, Jim. I've got a cab coming. I just called for one."

"You *called* a cab? You can hail one faster. The called ones never come. C'mon, where you going? I can run you over to the paper."

She hesitated, then got in.

"What's wrong with your car?"

"I wish I knew. Won't turn over."

"I'll drop you at the paper, from a block away if you're worried someone will see." She smiled. "And then I'll come back here and take a look. Can't be anything serious. Has it been acting up?"

"Not at all."

"Probably nothing big then."

"Oh, Jim, no. I can't let you do that. I'll get a garage to look at it tomorrow. If you can just run me to my office, someone can take me home, and I'll work it out, no problem."

"Forget it. By the time you're off work, I'll be back to pick you up and take you to your car. Fair enough?"

"I really can't let you do that. It's sweet of you, but no."

"C'mon! My one chance to be a white knight? Don't ruin it for me. Don't forget, I'm gonna be Officer Friendly."

She laughed and removed her car keys from her key ring for him. He chided her. "That's right. Hang onto those apartment keys, just like Officer Friendly would advise. Too easy to copy."

When she got off work that night, she hoped Bobby—a sweet kid, but a climber and sometimes a big mouth—didn't notice that Jim was waiting out in front. Jim took her back to her car and explained the minor problem that had interrupted the ignition. She thanked him profusely. He asked if he could see her again since he wouldn't be seeing her on business much any more.

"I shouldn't," she said.

"If I was still going to see you every night on duty, I might not have asked you this soon."

"I'd better not."

"You'd better."

"I don't know."

"I won't beg."

"I wouldn't want you to."

"Please, oh please!"

And they both laughed. "You can call me," she said finally. "But no promises."

"Ah, so it depends on where I'm going to take you. How do you feel about professional wrestling?"

"Are you kidding?"

"Of course."

"Whew!"

"I was thinking more in terms of a concert at Ravinia."

"Now that I'd love," she said.

"Saturday?"

"Saturday."

There had been many Saturdays since then. And Sundays at his church. And hers. And Friday nights. And last night. He was perfect for what ailed her. He wasn't pushy. He wasn't demanding. He let her talk about Scott. He let her cry.

It almost embarrassed him that he grew to love his Officer Friendly role. "It's not something I want to do the rest of my life," he said, "because I'd still like to land in Homicide eventually, but I *do* like working with kids."

"I wouldn't think investigating homicides would be something you'd want to do the rest of your life either," she said.

"It wouldn't always be pleasant. But it would always be a challenge, and a worthy one. If we believe God is the author of life, we should want to oppose those who take lives." But she wondered what it would be like to be married to a man who dealt with bodies and blood and murderers all day.

Then she scolded herself for even thinking that way. What Jim Purcell did with his life was his business, and besides, they weren't past the hand-holding stage. No commitments had been made, no love expressed.

Did she love him? She could. She was capable. She might someday. But now? Did she? She wasn't sure. She figured she'd know when she did. She knew one thing: she loved to watch him with kids. With his Sunday school kids, his friends from church. Even with her nieces and nephews.

And though people in both churches and both families had started making assumptions, she and Jim had not even said they wouldn't see other people yet. No one from their respective places of work knew anything about their relationship. They liked each other. A lot. And she thought he probably loved her. He had expressed it in many ways. She missed him when she didn't see him. She was happier when she was with him.

Sounds like love, she thought. *Feels like love*. But she had been through it before. And the loss, even the potential of the loss of one she could hold so dear, scared her, slowed her, made her careful.

Now, as she entered the Sixteenth Precinct on what she sensed was as important a day in police news since she'd been on the beat, she was thinking of Jim and the quiet dinner they had enjoyed. Simultaneously, she reached into her bag for her note pad.

"Good evening, Herb," she said to Flannigan. "What've you got? Who can I see?"

"Nothin' and nobody. How's that?"

She started to smile, but he wasn't kidding. "What's the matter, Herb? Is everything under wraps? You must know by now who was hit. Anybody I know?"

"I can't tell you anything. It's a guy from IAD, and he's brass. He's at Henrotin, and if you tell anybody I tol' you, it's the last thing you'll ever get from me."

"I appreciate it, Herb. You know I do. Now what was the bust?"

"I'm afraid it was right here in the Sixteeth," he said. "And I'm serious, I can't say a word. I wouldn't tell you who if you paid me."

"Campbell in?"

"He's in, but the official answer is no, if you know what I mean."

"No way he'll see me?"

"No way."

Jennifer pursed her lips and headed for the pay phone near the stairs. "Hi, it's Grey," she said. "Let me talk to Leo."

While she waited for Leo, she was tempted to try Jim at home again and, short of that, asking Flannigan if Jim had been called in for emergency duty.

"Yeah, Jenn!"

"Leo, I'm at the Sixteenth and getting nothing. I'm going over to Henrotin where they've got this Chief of Internal Affairs."

"Lucas?"

"Is that his name?"

"'Course that's his name. You don't have your department directory with you?"

"No."

"John Lucas. Very big name. Very impressive. Big news if he's been hit. You know this for sure? I'll start a bio."

"I can't be sure yet if it's Lucas, but it sounds like he's in pretty bad shape, whoever he is. You think I'll get anybody in Public Information this time of night?"

"I doubt it, but it's worth a try. I can only hold page one until three A.M., and I mean three. You call me at quarter to with whatever you've got, and I gotta tell ya, it better be more than you've got now. You know how many were busted?"

"No."

"Better get to Henrotin. We'll get the arrested officers from the TV or the wires. Concentrate on the shot cop, and Bobby'll track down the rest."

I bet he will, Jennifer thought, feeling as if she had failed already. She didn't want help. She didn't want to be reminded what she'd forgotten. She didn't want to have to concentrate on just one aspect of the story, regardless of the time pressure. She was mad.

Pushing open the glass door to the lobby she called to Flannigan. "Give me the number for Public Information, fast!"

He didn't have time to think about it. He peeled open the dog-eared department directory and yelled out the number. When the switchboard downtown answered, Jennifer identified herself and asked for the Public Information Director. "No, it's not an emergency," she said with more sarcasm than she should have.

She was told he was unavailable. "Are you telling me he's not in the office? Because I don't think his wife will be too thrilled to take a call right now, especially if he isn't home."

"He's here, but unavailable."

"Tell him it's the *Chicago Day* and don't tell me he isn't out talking to the broadcast people right now. Tell him I just need him for a second."

Jennifer looked at her watch and panicked. If she was just getting information that Bobby could get elsewhere and she missed the one part of the story Leo told her to stay on, she'd be in big trouble. She tapped her foot impatiently and began preparing herself to run to her car as soon as she talked to the Public Information Director.

"This is Nelson, sir. What is it?"

"First of all, I'm not a sir, but don't apologize. I'm Jennifer Grey with the *Day* and—"

"Yes, I've seen your stuff—"

"Good, I need to know what Sixteenth Precinct officers were arrested this morning."

"I'm sorry, Grey, but those announcements don't come from this office. They are always handled by Internal Affairs, and I'm afraid they're incapacitated at this moment."

"Because John Lucas is in intensive care at Henrotin?"

"Who told you that?"

"You did. I was just guessing. Thanks, Nelson."

"You're welcome."

"Just one more thing. Where are the arrested officers being booked?"

"Down here."

"Can I come?"

"Suit yourself. But we won't even be giving out the names."

You might not be, Jennifer thought, *but somebody down there is always eager to tell what they know.*

Four

Jennifer sped to Henrotin Hospital on the Near North Side and debated parking in the emergency lane. Instead, she parked as close as she could to the door and popped her press card on the dash. *That's one way to beg for a ticket,* she thought.

She was among the press latecomers in the emergency room, asking all the questions everyone else had already tried. And getting the same answer. No comment. She walked the halls and asked doctors, nurses, aides, and custodians if they knew anything at all about the condition of the man in intensive care.

They had been briefed well. That or they'd been through this before, Henrotin being a popular site for the most common emergencies in the world of crime that surrounded it. Jennifer spotted a pay phone and dialed the emergency room. She could hear the nurse on duty live in one ear and by phone in the other. She turned toward the wall so the effect wouldn't be reversed.

"This is Jennifer Grey calling from the Near North Side," she said. "I must know immediately if you called the morgue and whether you will be transferring Mr. Lucas's body there?"

"I didn't call the morgue," she said. "I don't believe Mr. Lucas has expired, ma'am."

"Is that correct? I understood that he may have already died."

"One moment please."

A male voice came on. "This is Dr. Burris. May I help you?"

"I need to know the condition of Mr. Lucas as soon as you can put me in touch with someone in authority."

"Well, we'll be releasing this to the press at about three-thirty A.M. anyway if there has been no change: His condition is grave. He is suffering from wounds to the abdomen and the cardiovascular system. He has not been conscious since the time of the shooting. We have been able to remove only one bullet at this time, and further surgery must be postponed until his condition stabilizes, probably not for several hours. All vital signs are weak."

"What kind of chance would you give him, Doctor?"

"One in ten."

"Thank you."

Jennifer phoned the news in to Leo and headed downtown. There'd be no one falling for an innocent phone call down at headquarters, however straightforward. She had never been able to justify lying, which Leo felt was fair. She always told the party her name and what she wanted to know, emphasizing the urgency of it and appealing to their rank. If they asked her more specifically why she wanted to know, she told them, but they seldom asked.

Jennifer arrived at 2:30 A.M. Again she was a latecomer. Her colleagues pressed around Public Information Director Nelson, who was asking how many were on a hot deadline. "I am," Jennifer called, remembering the days when it was all she could do to muster the courage to ask a simple question at a press conference.

"I oughta head for the phone right now," one of her competitors quipped. The *Day* stayin' open after sundown is front page stuff!"

Everyone guffawed, but Jennifer ignored them and talked directly to Nelson again. "I'm looking at fifteen minutes," she said. "I'll take whatever you've got."

"All I have is four names."

"We've all got the names," she said, taking a chance, assuming Leo and Bobby had been able to get that much. She lost the gamble. Everyone turned and stared, then shouted at Nelson, demanding to know why she had information that they didn't.

He held up both hands. "She's bluffing," he said. "No one has the names because I just got them myself. Now, Grey, the names are all I have except a few details. If you've already got what I'm about to give, you might as well head back to the *Day*. " She stared him down.

"Now, then, ladies and gentlemen, a few ground rules. I have very brief, very sketchy reports for you. I will read them verbatim the way I have been instructed. I will not be able to comment further on them. I have nothing more on the arrests themselves, and I cannot release the names of the arresting officers.

"I can tell you that at around midnight, the Internal Affairs Division of the Chicago Police Department made four arrests of police personnel, charging them with trafficking in controlled substances. These four arrested officers are being held without bail in this facility. The police commissioner is releasing the following statement: 'These arrests come after lengthy preparation by the Internal Affairs Division. However, we will consider the arrested officers innocent until proven guilty. Any so found will not only be dismissed from the police force but will be prosecuted to the full extent of the law.'

"That statement was prepared in advance. With the wounding of IAD Chief John Lucas, the commissioner has added this: 'Our prayers are with the wounded officer and his family.'

"Lucas's is the only name I can give you from the list of arresting officers. He was critically wounded during the arrest of Lieutenant Frank Akeley of the Sixteenth Precinct. The arrest was made in the parking lot of The Illusion bar on Wells Street. I know none of the details except that Chief Lucas was hit three times by small caliber ammunition and is in intensive care at Henrotin Hospital at this time. No one else was injured."

"Did this Akeley shoot him?"

"I am not at liberty to comment on that."

"How many officers were at the scene?"

"I do not know."

"Is he expected to live?"

"I'm sorry, gentlemen and ladies. As I told you, this is all I have. Now there is more on the other arrests, if you'd care to hear it."

"Yeah, but you got stats on Akeley?"

"Yes. White, male, age fifty-nine, five feet eleven inches, one hundred eighty-five pounds. The highest ranking officer arrested this evening. An employee of the City of Chicago for thirty-two years."

"Family?"

"That's all I have."

"Stats on Lucas?"

"'Yes. White, male, age fifty-six, six feet two inches, one hundred ninety pounds. Thirty-year employee."

"Family?' "

"Wife, four grown daughters."

"The other arrested officers included Sergeant William Much, also Sixteenth Precinct. Arrested at his home on the West Side. He's married, two teenage sons and a younger daughter. White, male, age forty-three, six feet four inches, two hundred sixty-five pounds. Employed by Chicago PD for nineteen years."

"Who arrested him?" Laughter.

"I don't have that information."

"Is the arresting officer still alive?" More laughter. Nelson ignored it.

"That name sounds familiar. Has he ever been up on charges before?"

"No, but we've released stories about him from our office twice in the last year. One—which none of you used—was a feature on the fact that he's our singing policeman. The other—which you all used—was that he was our biggest policeman and that he had been ordered to lose weight before the end of this year."

"How's he doing? He gonna make it?"

Nelson was not amused. He looked as if he wanted to say he didn't have that information, but of course he had the file on the old feature story. He ignored the question anyway.

"Arrested on duty, and again, I am not at liberty to give you the name of the arresting officer, was Patrol Officer Trudy Janus, white, female, age twenty-seven, five feet five inches, one hundred forty pounds. Single. Employed here three years."

"First female in that precinct?"

"Yes."

"First female officer ever arrested?"

"I believe so. Better not quote me on that."

"Any of these resist arrest?"

"No comment."

"Did more than one resist arrest?"

"No."

"There's one more?"

"James Purcell, a specially assigned Patrol Officer, white, male, age twenty-nine, six feet one inch, one hundred seventy pounds, six-year employee. Arrested at his Near North Side apartment."

Jennifer squinted and stared unblinking at Nelson. Her throat had tightened at the first mention of Jim's name, and her desperate hope that it was another James Purcell was dashed immediately with the cold recitation of his statistics. The numbness that had plagued her after the death of her husband swept over her once more.

There has to be a mistake, she thought as she stiffly backed away from the scene. She was terrified for Jim and what he must be going through. She didn't want to face the news. It was too stark, too impersonal, too awful. It took her back three years to the phone call that asked her if she were Mrs. Scott Alan Grey. She knew by the way she had been asked that something terrible had happened.

The caller had identified himself as a state trooper and asked cordially if she would be home for the next half hour or so and could he please drop by for a moment. She had known so certainly then that she called her father and told him to come to Arlington Heights, that Scott had been killed, and that she needed her parents.

She never once doubted the truth of her conviction, and, of course, she was right. She made it easy on the young trooper. "How did it happen?" she asked, refusing his suggestion that she sit down.

"Multiple car accident, icy roads. No one's fault."

"Anyone else hurt?"

"Yes, ma'am. No other fatalities, however."

"Could you stay with me for a half hour or so until my parents arrive?"

"Of course. Would you like me to call them for you? It wouldn't be any trouble."

"They're on their way."

Jennifer's first thought as she backed through the door now was to stop at the pay phone and call her father. But she couldn't. There were too many reasons she couldn't. She wanted to shut this out, to wake up from it, to be done with it.

Her deadline was closing in, and she was a newspaper woman. She was not a woman in love. She was not a person with a second chance at life. She was Leo Stanton's ace police reporter. Maybe she had wobbly legs, and maybe she was on the verge of hysterics. But a grown woman doesn't wake up her father in the middle of the night when she has a job to do.

So she phoned Leo. While the rest of the pack were running for other phones and howling about Officer Friendly being a dope dealer and "Wasn't this the guy who wanted out of vice control because he wasn't old enough? No, he found out there wasn't as much money in it!" Jennifer told Leo that he'd better get another hour from the pressmen.

"I told you, Jenn, three means three. We go to press in a few minutes. What's the matter with you anyway? You sound strange."

"I'm sitting on the biggest story of my career, Leo. Trust me. I'll come straight in and give you a lead story for page one in the first draft. If you don't hold the press for this piece, we'll be blown out by all the other news media."

"You know what you're asking, Jennifer?"

"Leo, I asked myself what you would do in this situation, and that's what I'm doing."

Stanton laughed a rueful laugh. "I can't argue with that. I'll get you a four o'clock pressrun; you get in here and give me the story."

Jennifer knew she couldn't drive, so she grabbed a cab and paid him in advance so she could jump out when he slid up to the night entrance at the *Day*. She hid her face in her hands and tried to control her sobs, but she couldn't.

The public has a right to hear this story whether these people are guilty or innocent, she told herself over and over. *He just has to be innocent! He couldn't! He wouldn't! I know him too well! Who am I kidding? I don't know him at all. I've been taken. He used me. But the story can't be vindictive. It has to be straight. It has to be the piece I would write if I'd never heard of the man. God, don't let this be true! Please make it all be a mistake!*

She hurried into the city room, shedding her coat and her bag and reading her notes as she walked. Bobby approached and handed her a story. "Leo let me take a shot at the Lucas piece. What do you think?"

She sensed Bobby's gloating and tried to scan the piece through her tears.

> John Lucas, 56, is fighting for his life at Henrotin Hospital this morning after suffering multiple gunshot wounds during a midnight arrest on the Near North Side.
>
> The long-time veteran with a reputation for incorruptibility was personally handling the arrest of Chicago Police Lieutenant Frank Akeley, 59, who allegedly opened fire in the parking lot of . . .

"Yeah, yeah, I think that'll be OK," Jennifer managed, wondering which story Leo would lead with. Not that she cared. In a selfish, protective way, she could wish that he would bury her story. She would beg him to leave her name off it, maybe even threaten to quit if he didn't comply.

Leo gave her a puzzled look, and she slowed as she passed his desk, wondering if she didn't owe him some sort of an explanation. He started to pull his cigar from his lips, then remembered the time and just left it.

He clicked his fingers and pointed to her video display terminal, and she kept walking.

It was warm in the city room, or was it just Jennifer? She pulled her sweater over her head and sat, still steaming, in her blouse. She set up her note pad next to the machine while trying to remove her boots with her free hand. No luck.

She bent down and put her head under the desk to get a better vantage point from which to attack the zippers. While in that ridiculous position, it hit her what she was about to do.

She was going to write a story for the fastest growing newspaper in Chicago that would end a man's career forever, guilty or innocent. *But the story won't, can't, say he's guilty,* she reasoned.

And the facts will be broadcast on radio and television and printed in all the other papers anyway. There's no way I can protect him. And why should I? Because I know he can't be guilty, that's why, don't I? And either way, its a story. A valid story. Either way, it's news that he was arrested. And there's irony in his present assignment.

She had to do it. Leo stared at her taking so long to take off her boots. She'd been running since Bobby had called her just before 1:00 A.M. She needed a shower. She needed a shampoo. She needed a change of clothes. She needed a bed.

What she wanted was her parents. *Why do I have to be such a baby?* Her dad had told her that it took more of a woman to admit she needed someone than to need someone and pretend she didn't.

That was sage advice, as usual, from Dad. But this time it didn't fit. Because this time what she wanted and what she needed were two different things. She would have said to herself, and did, that she wanted her parents. She wanted to go home to Rockford, home to her old bedroom, home to long days of sleeping her cares away.

But what she needed? What she really needed? If she'd had her choice of all the options in the world, would she really go home? No. She would go to Jim. She would tell him she believed him, whatever his story was.

And she knew when she even let that thought enter her head that it was ludicrous. It was the thought of a crazy woman. It was the kind of thing a woman in love would say. *I love him,* she told herself. *I finally know that I love him, and I have every reason to believe he's a criminal.*

Surer of her love than of his innocence, she straightened up, gave one hard glance back at Leo who had been about to tell her to make good on her page one story or hit the bricks—and turned to her machine.

Her tears began afresh, and as they rolled down her face, she punched in the toughest story she would ever write. Knowing it would go out over the *Day* syndicate as well, she datelined it Chicago and began:

> James Purcell, 29, the Sunday school teaching Chicago policeman who begged off from his unsavory assignment to the Vice Control Division early this year and has been serving as Officer Friendly in areas schools, was one of four 16th Precinct police officers arrested early this morning and charged with buying and selling illegal drugs.
>
> In the quadruple arrests that took place at four separate locations simultaneously, Internal Affairs Division Chief John Lucas was critically wounded. (See separate story.) The other three arrests, including Purcell, veteran Sergeant William Much, 43, and Patrol Officer Trudy Janus, 27, were without incident....

Five

It was all Jennifer could do to finish the article, she wanted so badly to see Jim.

But at the lockup she was faced with a brick wall. "No, Jennifer, absolutely not, no way. Sorry."

"What're you talking about, Bradley?" she pleaded with the lanky, dark deskman. "You've taken me in to see your *own* prisoners before!"

"Maybe that's why I got stuck on desk duty, Jenn. I've got orders. Nobody sees these four except their lawyers. That's it, so don't beg."

"Can you give him a message for me?"

Bradley appeared to consider it. "Not without clearance from my boss, Jennifer."

"How long would that take?"

"I dunno. He works the day shift, and I ain't gonna call him at home. I could leave it for him."

"Forget it," she said, trying to keep from screaming. "Is there really no way I can get in there for a few minutes, if I promise to keep your name out of it?"

"C'mon, Jennifer, I told you not to beg. I'm in charge of the keys until tomorrow, so there's no way anyone can keep my name out of anything if you get in there. I'm sorry, OK?"

Jennifer couldn't speak, not even to thank him for listening to her. She trudged to her car, fighting tears and suddenly feeling the fatigue that the last few hectic hours had made her ignore. She banged both hands against the steering wheel, fighting the sobs that were just beneath the surface.

She made a conscious decision not to cry. She wanted to be with Jim, but she couldn't be, and that was that. Sleep was what she needed.

The morning papers and the radio talk shows made the most of the arrests, speculating on how many police officers would wind up indicted when all the results were in.

They had great fun, of course, with the singing policeman—the biggest man on the force—being brought down by the scandal. But their ire was reserved for Jim Purcell, the one they said had played the "all-American boy" image to the hilt.

While hearts bled for John Lucas, and hourly hospital reports sounded worse and worse, Jennifer sat in her apartment unable to turn away from the radio call-in programs. People who knew nothing except what they'd read in the paper, and—she knew many of them had read only her article—ranted and raved about the fact that "this man, or at least this person who calls himself a man, spends his days telling kids that the police department is on their side and spends his nights selling heroin to the same children!"

Leo had reluctantly complied with her ultimatum, and she wondered if she would have had the fortitude to follow through with her threat to resign if he had crossed her. After hearing the diatribes all morning, she knew she would have. Still, even without the byline, Jim Purcell would know who wrote those stories.

And why was she still worried about that? If it had all been a mistake and he was cleared, he'd have to understand, wouldn't he? Wouldn't any sane adult know that the story was news? That it would have appeared everywhere else anyway? And that she and the *Day* would have looked suspicious for not covering it?

But the more she thought about it, the more she knew that it was something else that was bothering her. It was the possibility that it was all true. That she had been duped by a con man second to none. If she was wrong about Jim, she could never trust another human being as long as she lived.

The man was special. He reminded her of her own father. The kindness, the understanding, the gentleness, the insight. Could a person be that confused, that deceived, that totally swept away by someone?

It was inconceivable! She wracked her brain for clues to a side of him she never knew. He was idealistic. He was sometimes unrealistic. Yet he was responsible. He was one of those who volunteered for unpopular duty, working weekends and holidays when the family men wanted to trade days off.

Were there times when he was unavailable, and she didn't know why or he didn't explain? She could think of none. There seemed to be a lot of meetings, staff meetings. And not always at the precinct house. Could that have been when he was doing his dirty work? She had no reason to believe that.

No reason except for the sketchy reports coming out of Internal Affairs that this surveillance had been under way for longer than Jim had been in the precinct. She decided she could live with the bad news more easily

than with no news. If she could find out for sure that he was the scoundrel
the stories implied, she would deal with the pain, the remorse, the grief of
it, the same way she had dealt with the loss of Scott.

There were similarities; of course there were. Especially after the
realization at her keyboard in the wee hours that she was indeed in love
with Jim. Memories of their praying together stabbed through her. Could
he be a phony? Is it possible? Could a man drag God into a sham? I
suppose a real pro could.

But Jim was sincere in his distaste for the work he'd been assigned in the
Vice Control Division. Having to play up to prostitutes and pay off
informants. Deciding which crime was more important and letting the
small-time criminal go, and maybe even helping him or her out, in
exchange for the bigger prey.

He said he'd been raised straight and had never really been in serious
trouble, certainly not involving the seamier side of life. He was not only
repulsed by the after-dark world of Chicago, but he also found himself
fascinated and even tempted by parts of it. He found himself thinking
thoughts he'd never entertained before, seeing pictures in his mind he
wondered if he could ever erase.

He wasn't a prude, he'd said. It wasn't that he didn't know what went on
behind closed doors. But he'd always appreciated the counsel of an older
Christian policeman who had said that a Christian officer "must be fully
acquainted with sin but not partake of it."

This vice control business was for someone else, according to Jim. And
when Jennifer heard his view of it, she had to agree. There were bad,
horrible, awful sides to other parts of police work too—like trying to solve
grisly murders. But while they, too, left memory pictures that needed
cleansing, they didn't begin to work on a young man's imagination or
make him remember the alluring sights of the underworld. And only a
blind man could deny that they were there.

No man would admit to his family that he wanted all that went with the
action in the sleazy strip joints and hangouts. There was filth and disease
and burned-out men and women. But could the same man say that there
weren't sights that appealed to his lower nature, possibilities that excited
his fantasies?

Jim, Jennifer felt, had decided he didn't need that kind of input. He was
admitting to the world that it took either a stronger man for the work or
one who didn't care about the purity of his thought life.

Jim had told Jennifer more than he had told any other reporter because
he was telling her off-the-record as a friend, even though he never
stipulated such. He had told her that his reason was his faith in Christ, his
eagerness to do and to be and to become all that God wanted him to.

Somehow she couldn't make those lofty ideals fit the worst con man in the business. But maybe they were what made him the best.

She rose from the couch, where fits of exhausted sleep left her more tired than refreshed, and shuffled to the phone. She called Leo at home. "Well, I guess we've got another paper to put out for tomorrow morning," she said.

"Yeah, I suppose we do, Jenn. You all right?"

"I think so."

"We're going to have to talk about it, you know that, don't you?"

"Talk about what?"

"C'mon, Jenn. You're talking to Leo. And Leo knows. You ought to know that by now. But better than that, just like your mom, Leo cares. Thing is, you can snow Mom. You can't snow Leo."

"I know. I'm sorry."

"Don't be sorry. Just talk to me. What's happening with you, Jennifer? Why are you taking this story so hard? You get too close to these people or something? Know them too well? I warned you about taking sides, about seeing yourself as one of the cops instead of a reporter, standing between them and the readers."

"Yeah, well, maybe that was it, Leo. It does hurt to see people hurt."

"But they hurt people, Jennifer. It was their fault. You've got to see that, to separate yourself from them, to see the public's side. If you're going to be a bleeding-heart cheerleader for the cops, you're no good to us in your job."

"Maybe you're right. Maybe I'm no good in the job."

"We both know that's garbage. You called me. You said we've got another paper to put out. That tells me you're ready for an assignment today. I was going to give you a day off, but if you're ready—"

"You were? You were going to give me a break? I don't know what to think about that, Leo. What am I supposed to think about that?"

"Since when are you asking me what you're supposed to think? That'll be the day."

"No, I just mean, are you feeling sorry for me? Wondering if I can handle the job? What?"

"You worked hard last night, and it was getting to you. It showed. You can't deny that."

"It showed in my piece?"

"No, your story was as nice as you've done since you've been with me. But you do a great job, you cry at your desk, you don't want your name on the story. I'm no psychiatrist, Jenn, but I've got to think my star reporter needs a day to herself."

"That's thoughtful, Leo. But no, I think I'll do better working than sitting around here all day thinking."

"You're sure?"

"Yeah."

"You want an assignment?"

"Sure."

"You know it's going to be right in the middle of this Internal Affairs bust."

"Sure."

"Well, there have been a few developments I'd like you to check out. First, the names of the arresting officers have leaked out. Bobby's got 'em at the office. You can try to contact them. Second, Lucas has taken a turn for the worse. The doctors are saying it's only a matter of time. Third, no one but their lawyers is allowed in to see the four busted cops, but get this: only three of them even have lawyers. Akeley, who's been formally charged now with resisting arrest, assault with a deadly weapon, and attempted murder, has procured this Williams, you remember the guy?"

"The Williams who represented the City of Chicago in federal court? Big stuff."

"Yeah, that's the guy. But I have a feeling that with the testimony of two of his own precinct cops against him, Akeley's going to need more than Williams. Anyway, it appears this Bill Much, the—"

"Sergeant."

"Yeah, Much is broke and is using a public defender. That's worth a few laughs when you think about it. A defender of the public violates the public trust, then hires a public defender to defend himself against the public. It's too good. But not funny. I'm sorry. I forgot how you're reacting to this."

"It's all right."

"OK, Janus has a guess-what lawyer?"

"A woman."

"You got it."

"A known feminist defender."

"Right again."

"You're telling me the fourth defendant doesn't have counsel yet?"

"That's the story, Jenn. He isn't going to have counsel. What's his name?"

"Purcell."

"Right. This James Purcell, the Holy Joe, has waived his right to a lawyer."

"Temporarily, surely."

"Maybe. But what's his game? That's what I want you to find out. What would you think of visiting his church? Talking to his pastor, some of his friends? They'll say they're shocked and all that, never would have thought it. Maybe they'll stick up for him. But go deeper. Find out what the parents of the kids he teaches in Sunday school think about letting their kids stay in his class if he gets out on bond. Or if the church will let him keep his class. What do the people think? I don't suppose you could get to one of the kids, but that would be interesting too. My guess is the kids will not believe it yet."

"Do you believe it, Leo?"

"I missed that."

"Do you believe Purcell is guilty?"

Leo swore. "They're all guilty, Jenn. Once in a great while there'll be smoke with no fire. But when you're talking official corruption, your cops and your politicians and your government employees, huh-uh. In the *Day*, just like in every other rag that wants to be fair and ethical, our pieces will be full of alleged this and allegedly that and all the rest. But let me tell you something: the alleged Akeley who allegedly shot the alleged chief of the alleged IAD is going to be in a heap of alleged trouble if his victim allegedly dies. Yeah, Jenn, they're all as guilty as sin, and when you've been on this beat long—in fact, probably after this coverage right here—you'll never doubt it again."

Jennifer was silent, trying to keep from crying.

"C'mon, Jennifer. Be realistic. I don't want to be such a cynic any more than anyone else, but you've got to snap out of this Pollyanna business. I like a reporter who can be optimistic and look on the bright side of things. But there is no bright side to a cop scandal. Talking to a guy's Sunday school class might seem a little crass. But did you ever see a story of a mass murderer that doesn't carry quotes from the people he grew up with, people who taught him?"

"I guess not."

"Of course you didn't. Now what do you want to take today? You get first choice of course. Bobby and I'll take the rest, along with a couple stringers we're borrowing from the newsroom."

"I'll tell you what I want to do, if you don't mind, Leo. I'd like to take you up on your offer of a day off. I could really use the time."

This time Leo was silent.

"Is that OK?"

"Sure, Jenn. How much time you need?"

"Just a day. I'll see you tomorrow afternoon."

"You going to get some rest, kid?"

"I don't know. I might go see my parents in Rockford."

"I'll be thinking about you. Give me a call if you need me, huh?"

"Thanks, Leo. Thanks a lot."

Six

Though she was hounded by it all the way up the Northwest Tollway, Jennifer couldn't decide what significance there was to Jim's decision not to procure a lawyer. Was it lack of money? Could she help? Should she? Would she have to quit her job first? What if she was wrong about him and quit her job to help him, all in vain? They'd both be ruined.

She wouldn't have thought twice about sacrificing her career for him if he was innocent. But how could she be sure? What was she saying? That she loved him enough to sacrifice for him, yet she didn't know if he was innocent?

She saw the familiar postbox with her parents' names—George and Lillian Knight—and pulled into the drive, realizing immediately that she had made a mistake. She had forgotten that her mother had invited her older brother, Drew, his nagging wife, Francene, and their three toddlers for a week.

Drew she loved. Francene she tolerated, trying to forgive her nasal twang (a gift from birth) and her constant badgering of her husband and the kids by blaming it on the burden of trying to manage such a household.

Tolerating Francene was a full-time job even without the kids crying, wetting, fighting, and running through every conversation in the house. When Jennifer's mother and dad saw her in the driveway, they ran out.

Her mother had that look of joy that accompanies the thought of having most of her family together. "Hi, honey," she called, embracing Jennifer. "Now if only Tracy could be here!"

George Knight, however, had the concerned look that went with having read the *Morning Star* and knowing something about his daughter that he had not yet told his wife. And Jennifer could tell.

"How are you, Jenny?" He asked, taking her hands in his and looking deep into her eyes. He was the only person who called her Jenny anymore, and it always transported her back to treehouses and sandboxes and long walks in the woods. He called her Jenny right through high school when they had their one-on-one talks that would go till after midnight.

He'd never said she was his favorite, but she knew. And he loved her, he always said, even when she was ornery. That always got to her. She'd be mean or terrorize her mother with that temper of hers, and he would sit her down and give her the Dutch uncle routine. She'd sulk and pout and refuse to admit she'd been wrong. She'd try the silent treatment, defying him with her eyes, and he'd say in a way that endeared him to her forever: "You can't make me not like you, Jenny Knight. And you can't stay mad at your old dad because I love you even when you're ornery."

And if she'd been so mean that she couldn't force a smile, she'd break down and cry, and he'd hold her. He never forced an apology out of her. But after she had seen herself in contrast to this sensitive, gentle man, she wanted more than anything to be like him, to get things right again, to forgive and forget and be forgotten.

Now he was staring into her eyes and asking her how she was, and she knew he knew what was going on. Somehow she sensed that he had not told the others. Mom wasn't a newspaper reader, unless Jennifer had written the story. Drew was way above front-page news, always with his nose in some science magazine. And Francene hadn't sat still long enough to read a paragraph since her firstborn, her four-year-old wonder, had come along.

"Oh, Drew!" came the dreaded whine. "Look who's here! Hi, Jennifer. How are you?"

Jennifer saw her father's face soften into an understanding smile. She rolled her eyes. "Hi, Fran! Good to see you."

"How long can you stay?" Mrs. Knight wanted to know.

"Not long," Jennifer said, having wished she could stay overnight, but realizing now that it would do her psyche and her problem no good to try to survive a houseful of relatives.

"Well, come in and sit down," her mother said. "Have a bite."

Drew pecked her on the cheek as she came through the door, and he rounded up all the kids to say hi to Aunt Jennifer. They came, kicking and screaming, performing their duties and heading off to see what more havoc could be wreaked.

When her mother was at the stove, Jennifer's father leaned close. "Where's your head?" he whispered.

"Right here," she said, pointing to her heart. He nodded with an I-thought-so look. "I forgot they were going to be here," she said, and he nodded again. "What I really need, Dad, is a long talk with you."

"I think we can work that out," he said. "What do you think, Mom?"

"What's that, dear?"

"You think Jenny and I could sneak away for an hour or so before dinner?"

"Sure. Be back by five-thirty though."

The frozen path that led to the woods behind the house seemed so much smaller than it had the last time they had walked there. Fatigue had set in, and Jennifer needed to rest. They sat on dry stumps in the middle of a tiny alcove, and she wondered aloud what her mother would think when she read about Jim.

"Let me worry about that," her father said. "I'm more concerned with what you're thinking right now."

So she told him. The whole story. How she heard. What she felt. What she did. What she said to Leo. That she knew she loved Jim, and mostly, that she was surer of her love than of his innocence.

She had finished, and, as was her father's custom, he didn't respond immediately. He just sat. Thinking. Waiting. Giving her a chance to restate anything she had not said the way she wanted to. Letting her own words echo in her ears to see how they sounded out in the open rather than in the echoing valleys of her mind.

She wasn't tempted to ask him what he thought. She knew he'd tell her. When he had sifted it through, he would ask her a few questions she hadn't thought to ask herself. He would give her insight she could have had on her own. He would lead her to her own decisions, never trying to force one on her.

It hadn't always been that way. He wasn't perfect. He had tried so hard to hold on to her when she was an adolescent that he had, a time or two, tried to push his will onto her. It never worked, and they both learned from it. But he was so eminently forgivable, if for no other reason than that line about loving her even when she was ornery.

"What will it do to your love for him if you find that he's guilty?" he said at last.

Jennifer couldn't answer. As she had silently predicted, it was something she hadn't considered. His guilt she had considered. How would it affect her feelings for him? She had assumed, she thought, that her love for him was dependent upon his character.

"I think I love the man I thought he was," she said. "Does that make sense?"

"Do you think it does?"

"I know it sounds conditional, but that was all I knew of him. You can only love what you know, can't you?"

"Can you?"

"I learned things about Scott after we were married, and I loved him in spite of some of those."

"And vice-versa?"

"Of course. But, Dad, those were little things. Irritations, idiosyncrasies. Not character things. Not dishonest things."

He looked at her without speaking.

"I'm saying my love is conditional, aren't I?"

He smiled.

"Can't my love be conditional? Is there something wrong with falling out of love if you've been betrayed, if someone is not only not what you thought they were, but the exact opposite?"

"Are you asking me or telling me?"

"I'm asking you, Dad, but I know how you counsel. You'll tell me it's not what you think that matters, but what I think. But I'm so confused right now that I need some feedback from you. What kind of crazy lady doesn't know she loves someone until he's in trouble? I mean, I know now that I was in love with him before without realizing it. But why does it hit me with such force when it appears he's everything I hate in a person?"

"You're not loving him because he's in jail, Jenny. You're loving him for the same reason you loved him those last few times you brought him up here."

"You knew?"

"Of course, we could tell. You can't hide something like that. Other people always know before the stricken one knows. But now maybe you know for sure because he needs you. If he was hurt or missing or victimized in some other way, it would have hit you the same way. It's not so paradoxical as it seems."

"But what will it do to my love for him if I find out he's guilty?"

"That question sounds familiar."

"He could be, you know, Dad."

"He could be guilty?"

"Of course. The odds are that he is. They've been watching that precinct for so long. They don't make arrests like that without something solid. Oh, I've been through all this."

"That's all right. You'll go through it a lot more before you come to any conclusions, honey. You'd better just keep kicking it around in your head until it settles into place."

"If I had to answer you now—"

"Which you don't."

"I know, and I appreciate that. But if I had to answer you now, I'd say that finding out he was guilty would spoil my love for him. My love is built on trust and faith. If he had fallen, made a mistake, taken a wrong turn, that would be one thing. I think I could love him through that. But if he's been involved in this since before we met and has been living a lie before me all this time—then, no, that would be the end."

"You couldn't forgive him?"

"Ah, touché. I don't know."

Her father fell silent again.

"I know that's what God would do, Dad. But I'm not God."

"No, none of us are God. But we're supposed to be imitators of Him."

"You are."

"I'm not, Jenny. But it is my goal."

"Mine too. But I'm not there. I can't judge Jim. I can't know his heart, his motives, his sincerity. I'm afraid if I knew he was guilty, that he had been thumbing his nose at my pure love and I don't apologize for calling it that—then I would find it very difficult to accept an apology. Unless it was somehow very convincing."

"What does that make you think of, Jenny?"

"I know."

"Do you ever wonder if God believes you're sincere after you've, what did you call it, thumbed your nose at His pure love?"

"Yes. And there were times when I knew I wasn't sincere, and I knew He knew it, and it made me feel so guilty that I got sincere real quick."

George Knight smiled broadly and wrapped an arm around his daughter's waist as they walked back. "You've got a lot of thinking to do, girl." She nodded. "I do have one little bit of advice for you, though."

She stopped, surprised. "This is a switch."

"I won't say anything if you don't want me to," he said, "but I believe you really are confused and at the end of yourself. I don't mind telling you, I haven't seen you this troubled since—"

"Since Scott."

"Yes."

"I want your advice, Dad. Whatever it is, I want it."

"I can't tell you whether Jim is guilty or innocent. No one can. That will have to be proven. But all I want to tell you—and you can throw it out or take it or whatever you want—is that I think you'll handle this thing better if you give Jim the benefit of the doubt until you know for sure."

"I might look like a fool in the end."

"Maybe. But if he's a phony, he's already made a fool of you. And you'll have a lot of company. I like the man. Your mother likes him. The people in his church love him. You love him. If he's betrayed us all, then you can know it and go on from there.

"But what if he hasn't, Jenny? You can only gain by giving him the benefit of the doubt. Believe with all your heart that he's innocent. That there's an explanation. That it'll all work out in the end. If you're wrong, you were just prolonging how wrong you'd been from the start. But if you're right, you'll be glad you stuck by him."

They walked on in silence for several minutes. "My boss says the opposite, you know," she said finally.

"Doesn't surprise me. But he's talking to you as a newspaper woman. What was his line? Where there's smoke and all that? That's true enough. We both know the odds are against you. You said it yourself. You do your reporting job the best way you know how. But as God's person, as my daughter, as Jim's love, you believe in him until you're proven wrong. It's a much better angle from which to work, don't you think?"

"Don't I think? No, why should I think when I've got a dad like you to do my thinking for me?" And she hugged him.

When they got to the backyard, Lillian Knight was at the door. "Jenn! Your boss called. Wants you to call him right away. Say's he sorry to bother you, but it's urgent."

Seven

In person, Leo Stanton ranted and raved and used his expressions and gestures to make his points. On the phone, when he was really angry, he was tense, cold, impersonal.

"Jennifer," he said, "I think you'd better get back here as quickly as possible."

"What is it, Leo?"

"We can discuss it when you get here. When may I expect you?"

"You want me to leave right now?"

"I think that would be wise."

"Give me about an hour and a half then."

"Thank you," he said, hanging up without another word.

Jennifer tried to treat her fast departure as a minor crisis at the office, but in the car the mystery nearly drove her mad. Who did Leo think he was, demanding that she come back from her parents' without telling her what was going on? Had Lucas died? Did they simply need her at the office? Was that it? Couldn't he have just said that?

Maybe it was more. Maybe Leo had found out about her and Jim. She hoped not. That would ruin the plan that had been taking shape in her mind from the moment—just minutes before—when her father encouraged her to give Jim the benefit of the doubt.

She hadn't had time to sort it all out, but she agreed that taking the positive approach would save her—or at least postpone—a lot of grief. She'd be good for nothing in any effort to help clear Jim if she continually tormented herself with doubt.

She wanted to inform Leo of her chats with Jim—not of their relationship exactly, but of the discussions they'd had about his philosophy of life. She'd write these, she thought, in feature form, just providing curious readers with background on one of the arrested officers.

She didn't know what Leo would think. Worse, she didn't know what Jim would think. He didn't want a lawyer for some reason; maybe he didn't want her defending him either. Of course, he had told her all those things as a friend. But he hadn't ever *said* they were off-the-record, and he knew he was talking to a reporter, didn't he?

She knew she wasn't making sense, but this was something that could only help Jim. Readers who didn't believe him would have a field day—that's how she would sell it to Leo. A story about a guy who still maintains his innocence in the face of serious charges. Leo should love that.

All the while, of course, she would be hoping and praying that Jim's boyish honesty would come through and that someone would be convinced. Maybe the readers would get behind him again, the way they had when he took his stand against some of the things required of him as a Vice Control Division undercover cop.

But when Jennifer slowed to a stop and rolled down her window to toss money into the tollbooth basket, the frigid air brought her back to her senses, and she knew that Leo would see right through it. She was being naive. No one would buy it. If she was going to clear Jim, she'd have to do it with hard evidence.

But where would she get that? She didn't have access to the kind of information that would clear a man of a serious crime. Anyway, she hadn't even seen the evidence against him. What was she going to do if she found he'd been meeting with hoodlums or passing dope to kids in school yards?

She scolded herself again for thinking negatively. It wasn't going to be easy, following her father's advice. She usually assumed the worst in an effort to protect herself. She didn't want to get her hopes up anymore—not since Scott's life had been stolen from her.

That's the way she saw it. Someone had stolen Scott. She knew it was the enemy, the author of death, the one who comes to steal and to kill and to destroy. That supreme scoundrel had nearly ruined her life. She knew her God would be ultimately victorious and that He was still in absolute control. But she had learned a painful, bitter lesson from that loss. For as long as she was on this earth, she could take nothing for granted. She could look to a bright future, a time of consummation, an eternal home of peace. But she fought expecting too much from this present world.

That's why it took her so long to realize her true feelings about Jim. She was not only building her defenses against another disappointment. She was running full speed away from her feelings. She had enjoyed Jim. She had looked forward to seeing him. She had delighted in the quiet, peaceful, unpressured moments with him.

But she had not allowed herself to even consider that she might be falling in love with him. She wasn't blind. She knew what he was thinking, though he was cautious, sensitive, biding his time.

He wasn't pushy, wasn't rushing anything. She was amazed, when she thought about it, how childlike and innocent their relationship had been for so long—especially in this day and age (as her mother always said).

Perhaps he could have expected more from her. More encouragement. More affection. More response. It was clear theirs was not a brother-sister relationship; yet it could have appeared that way.

They told life stories, told secrets, told what they liked about each other. They walked hand-in-hand for hours, yet she worked hard—maybe too hard—at giving clues that said she was not open to an embrace or a kiss.

He'd been so understanding, though they never discussed it. It was one of the things she so appreciated about him. Could he sense that it was her loss that made her want to move so slowly, not just in the physical aspect, but in the whole area of commitment?

It wasn't that he made advances and then didn't act upset when she didn't respond. No, he could read her better than that. She didn't think she had been obnoxious about it; she had simply not encouraged it. And somehow, he understood.

With Scott, the relationship was probably typical, she thought. They liked each other. Then they missed each other. They wanted to be together. They talked about it, kidded about it, flirted, and joked about their marriage long before they had known each other well enough to be discussing it seriously. As they grew in their love, their jokes about being man and wife evolved into serious discussions of their plans.

Jennifer didn't know what she would have done if that same progression had begun with Jim. It would have put her off, certainly. She would have seen the similarities, known where it was leading, and she would have tried to jump off the carousel.

Not that she didn't care for Jim or had any reservations about him at all. But she was going to be careful this time. She was going to be sure; she was going to be realistic; she was going to be even a little fatalistic, though she had been counseled not to be.

Both her father and her pastor had told her that she wouldn't really protect herself by locking herself in a cocoon and insuring herself against another devastating disappointment. Both felt she would do better to concentrate on the tremendous odds—morbid though it might be to consider them—against someone suffering two such painful blows in one lifetime.

"Then you're saying that since it's so unlikely that I'd be twice widowed," she asked her pastor, "that I should just put it out of my mind and not worry about it?"

"I'm aware how unrealistic that has to sound to someone whose wound is so fresh," he had said. And she nodded. "And also coming from someone who has never suffered that kind of pain." And she nodded again, not intending to be cruel. "But Jennifer, you can survive this thing when you are able to pull yourself up and out of it with the help of your friends and your family and your God."

It had sounded so pompous and pietistic; and yet, as she mulled it over during the many hard months to follow, she saw the wisdom of it. She also knew the absence of anything else to say to the bereaved. The less said the better, she decided. She had learned, at least, how to best comfort grieving loved ones. You stand there, you hold their hand, you put your arm around them, you sit with them, you cry with them, you do something for them without offering or being asked, and you keep your mouth shut. Because when you say that you don't know what to say, you're proving just that. And when you think that there's nothing you can say that will change anything or assuage the grief, you are right on the money, and your quiet actions speak so much louder than your empty words that Jennifer almost missed her exit. *What's wrong with me?* she wondered. *Am I so worried about Leo that I'm burying myself in these gloomy thoughts?* She turned on an all-news radio station to hear if there was anything that would prepare her for Leo. After a few minutes, the city's most popular topic was in the news again.

> Two of the four police officers arrested just after midnight this morning have already been released on bond. Originally, no bond was set for the four, but attorneys for both Sergeant Wlliam Much and Patrol Officer Trudy Janus won emergency bond concessions late this morning, citing precedence in the previous police shakeup during which all charged officers had been released to the custody of their attorneys, pending hearings.

> No bond has been set in the case of Sixteenth Precinct Lieutenant Frank Akeley, who has been charged with the near fatal shooting of Internal Affairs Division Chief John Lucas during Akeley's arrest. Akeley's attorney, the noted municipal barrister, Carl Williams, has sought no concessions for his client at this point.

> The fourth arrested officer, specially assigned Patrol Officer James Purcell, has still not secured representation and has reportedly refused the offer of a

public defender. So though bond is apparently available for those officers who did not resist arrest, Purcell remains in the headquarters lockup at this hour.

There has been speculation that Frank Akeley's high-powered attorney might enter a self-defense plea and that counsel for Sergeant Bill Much may have already made overtures toward plea bargaining by offering his client as a state's witness.

The attorney for Ms. Janus, however, has released a statement that her client will be entering an emphatic not guilty plea.

In a related humorous note, if anything about this case can be considered funny, Jake Rogers, columnist for the *Chicago Day* writing in a special midday edition, has noted the irony of Singing Policeman Bill Much offering to continue to sing about his and his colleagues' roles in this latest scandal....

Jennifer had always enjoyed Jake's columns. Until today. Her personal involvement in this case made it impossible for her to see any humor in it. She wondered if she would have anyway. There was something terribly sad about whatever it was that caused people to leave their ideals and bring shame on themselves and their families and their coworkers.

She wondered what bond had been set. If it was less than $50,000, perhaps she could scrape together the 10 percent of that necessary to get Jim out.

Jennifer parked behind the *Day* building on Michigan Avenue, wishing she'd stopped by her apartment to pick up her notes. She didn't know if Leo wanted her to work or what. But by his tone on the phone, it could have been anything from a change of his mind to a new break in the story or even a true calling on the carpet. She hadn't faced his anger since that first week under his supervision, but his tongue lashings were legendary.

She planned to stop at the washroom mirror for one last peek, but she saw Bobby Block heading down the back hallway toward her.

"Hi, Jenn! Didn't know you were going to be in today."

"Neither did I. What's happening, Bobby?"

"In the big one? Not much. Lucas has stabilized, but the docs are still doubtful about his recovery. Still on machines and everything. The arresting officers' names are out. Everybody's got 'em. Can't imagine how long they thought they were gonna keep those quiet with all the uniformed guys they pulled in for assistance."

"Yeah, Leo told me when he called."

"Guess their days with Internal Affairs are just about over. You know, once all the other cops know—"

"Yes, I know."

"Guess your time with the *Day* is just about over too, huh?"

Jennifer eyed him warily. "What are you talking about, Bobby?"

"Leo didn't tell you a couple of them were in here today?"

"Who?"

"The arresting officers. The ones who busted that singing sergeant and the young 'all-American boy' type. They were with Leo and the big boss more'n an hour, showing them pictures and reports and stuff, as far as I could tell. Leo didn't tell me anything, but I'm guessing they were telling Leo and Cooper about you and that cop."

Jennifer was stunned, but chose to ignore Bobby's attack for the moment. "*Max Cooper* was in on it?" she said.

"Who'd you think I meant by big boss? Nobody around here bosses the publisher, do they?" He looked smug. After months of playing the dutiful subordinate, Bobby had sensed his opening and turned on her.

Jennifer looked at her watch. It had been an hour and forty-five minutes since she'd talked to Leo. "Gotta run, Bobby. But thanks a lot for the loyalty and for telling Leo about me."

He smiled condescendingly. "I didn't have to, Jennifer. But I would have."

She shot through the swinging doors to the newsroom and moved straight through to the city room. No one looked up from their desks, for which she was glad. She didn't want to appear rude, but she was late.

She unbuttoned her coat as she neared her desk and draped it on her chair on the way by, noticing several memos and a stack of mail. It hadn't seemed that long since she'd been in. Leo was at his desk in his window-enclosed office, pretending to edit copy, but she knew him too well for that.

He had seen her the minute she hit the city room, and his pencil hadn't moved since. She tried to take a few deep breaths and be ready for anything, but her anxiety caught up with her and left her huffing and puffing.

Forgetting to knock, she breezed into Leo's office with an apology for being late. "Ran into Bobby in the hall and shouldn't have stopped to talk."

Without standing when she entered—as was his custom—Leo motioned to a chair and took off his reading glasses. He looked at her with raised brows, his chin still lowered as if he could have just as easily stayed with his work. She fell silent, deciding on the safest course, but her chest heaved as she tried to catch her breath without gasping.

Leo leaned forward and slowly pulled his day-old unlit cigar from his cheek and laid it gently in his personal ashtray, one which hadn't ever seen an ash. He picked up the tray and placed it behind him on an overhanging bookshelf, out of consideration for her, Jennifer hoped.

He turned around again to face her and leaned back in his chair, putting his feet on the desk and his hands behind his head. With his slightly frumpy Ivy League look, sleeves rolled up and tie loosened, she couldn't help thinking what an archetypical newspaper editor he was. And how right now he was milking his authority over her for all it was worth.

She wanted to say, "Let's get on with it, Leo. What's on your mind?" But she wouldn't dare do that with Leo Stanton. And just when she thought she'd burst if he didn't get on with it, he spoke.

"You were running late, but you stopped in the hall to chat with Bobby."

"Yes, I shouldn't have. I'm sorry."

"It's all right. At least, it's understandable. I mean, he works for you. Admires you. Looks up to you. Aspires to be like you."

"Oh, I wouldn't say—"

"I'm not trying to flatter you, Jennifer. I'm trying to make a bigger point, because there's something about your stopping to talk with Bobby that *isn't* understandable. You know what that is?"

She shook her head.

"The fact that you would tell me that was why you were late. I'm your boss. You should try to impress me. You *do* try to impress me. And that's OK. I do the same thing with my boss. Only I do it in a different way.

"If I was late to a meeting with my boss, I'd tell him it was the traffic, or car trouble, or anything other than the truth if the truth were so lame that it made me look bad. Don't you think it made you look bad that you were late to what you have to know is a very important meeting with your boss because you lost track of the time?"

"Well, yes, that's why I told you I was sorry, and I really am. It was inexcusable, and I hope you'll forgive me."

"If it's inexcusable, how can I forgive you?"

"Leo, I don't understand. I'm sorry. You're right. I was wrong. It won't happen again. If you want the whole truth, frankly I was gently pumping Bobby to see what would make you call me back to work from a day off."

"*You* don't understand? I don't understand. You're not just so honest that you tell me the real reason you were late; you tell me *more*. I've always appreciated your honesty, Jenn. It's one of the many things I like about you."

"Thank you, Leo, but it's not like you to beat around the bush. It's apparent you're leading up to something."

"If you don't mind my saying so, Jennifer, it's your whole honesty kick that leaves me so disappointed in you today."

He paused as if expecting a reaction from her. She had decided to say nothing more until he got to his point. Leo's lips tightened and he slid his feet off the desk to the floor and sat forward again.

"Jennifer, Jennifer. Why didn't you tell me about you and James Purcell?"

Eight

"There was nothing to tell, Leo."

Her boss shook his head sadly and looked away from her, making her feel low. "A police reporter fraternizing with a police officer and there was nothing to tell? Tell me we never discussed the danger of this, Jennifer."

"Of course we have, but the man was one of my first contacts. He was desk officer at the Sixteenth when I started. And when he was reassigned to duty that would never be something I would cover, I didn't see the harm in seeing him."

"Do you now?"

"I guess, but—"

"You guess? Can you tell me that wasn't the reason you were crying over that article last night?"

"It was, but it didn't show in the piece, did it?"

"You shouldn't have written the article. You were biased. "

"But it didn't show."

"You think the man is innocent."

"And you think he's guilty, Leo. Doesn't that make you biased?"

"I have every reason to believe he's guilty. Everyone believes he guilty. Everyone but you."

"I hadn't planned to start seeing him, Leo. And I've never used him for information."

"But it had to color your view of the police, didn't it?"

"No, it didn't. It really didn't. I have no doubt that Akeley shot Lucas, and not out of self-defense. Much has all but admitted he was guilty by offering himself up as a state's witness. And Janus has been a pistol ever since she joined the force. Her involvement in this wouldn't surprise me."

"Me either, Jenn. I agree with you all the way down the line except in one specific case: your boyfriend. Your relationship *had* to affect your view of him. They're all guilty and he's not? How do you reconcile that? Because you know him? What if you knew the others and developed a little sympathy for them? What if you'd heard Bill Much singing "The Big Brown Bear" to a bunch of elementary school kids and knew he had a sixth grade daughter with braces and that he coached his boys through Little League? Then would you say, 'Well, Akeley shot a man and Trudy Janus is a pistol, but my boyfriend and good ol' Bill Much, they're innocent?' "

"You don't understand," Jennifer said quietly.

"I didn't hear you."

"You don't understand how well I know Jim."

"I don't? I don't think I *want* to understand how well you know him! I'm trying to figure out this little game of deceit about your relationship with him and how that all fits in with your church and Sunday school thing; now don't get real honest with me and tell me you're having an affair with the man."

"I'm not. Of course I'm not. We haven't even kissed."

Leo almost had to suppress a smile. "I don't want to hear all of it, Jennifer. If you church types carry on serious romantic relationships without even kissing, that's just too interesting. I'm telling you you deceived me by saying nothing about it. You should have told me the first night he picked you up from the office."

"You would have taken me off the police beat," she said slowly.

"Possibly."

"That would have been unnecessary."

"You see what's happened and you can say that? The man is the laughingstock of this town because of his fresh-scrubbed image and now being up on charges, and you tell me it isn't significant that my police reporter is a very close personal friend?"

"How do you know how close or how personal or how much of a friend? He helped me with my car one night, and we've dated a few times."

Leo stood. "Can't you see it's too late to try to snow me about this?"

"I've never tried to snow you!"

"No, but you don't tell me everything either, do you?"

"I didn't tell you about Jim because I was afraid you would misunderstand something that did not and is not and will not affect my work."

"You're right that I would have misunderstood. You're wrong that it isn't or won't affect your work."

"It didn't."

"Granted."

"It isn't."

"If you'd seen yourself hunched over your VDT and bawling your eyes out last night, you wouldn't say that."

"But Leo! The story didn't show it!"

"Granted."

"It won't affect me in the future; I can promise that. I can be objective."

"Wrong. You don't want to write a piece about the 'real' Jim Purcell? You're not tempted to try to unload a piece on me about some of the things he's said over the past several months that prove that he just couldn't be the man everyone thinks he is?"

Jennifer was stunned. It was as if Leo had read her mind. But she had finally decided against that strategy. "No," she said weakly.

"How many times have you dated Purcell?"

"I don't know. Quite a bit."

"How much is 'quite a bit?' "

"I don't know, Leo. What are you driving at?"

"You want to know how many times you've seen him since that night your car broke down in front of the Sixteenth Precinct?"

"Did I say that's where it broke down?"

"Am I wrong? Where did it break down?"

"You're right."

"Do you want me to tell you where you went that night and the next Saturday? And the weekend after that? And Monday evening before the arrest? You want me to tell you where you had dinner and how long you stayed there and whether he opened the door for you? You want to see pictures of yourself in the parking lot with him?"

Jennifer couldn't speak.

"I don't enjoy this, Jennifer. But I think you're going to regret not telling me that you've been seeing a man on your beat." And he sat back down, rolled his chair back to his credenza, pulled open a file drawer, and produced a manila envelope full of black and white photographs.

He spread them on the desk before him. Jim and Jennifer at Ravinia. Jim and Jennifer at the beach. At dinner. At a concert. At a ball game. In the parking lot of her apartment building. At her church. At his church. Everywhere but at her home.

"You want pictures of you in a car with him on the Northwest Tollway?"

She shook her head. Her face was hot. "So you had me followed. You found out about Jim, and you put a tail on me. That's low. But what do you see in your pictures? Anything out of line? Anything more than holding hands?"

Leo stood again and sat on the edge of his desk, staring down at Jennifer and slowly shaking his head. "Jenn, you can't really think I'd do that. That's not me. I would have confronted you. I haven't the time or the money to put a tail on you. For what reason would I do that? To build some sort of a case against you? If I had known, I would have taken you off the beat, that's all. You wouldn't have been able to talk me into leaving you on. You wouldn't have been able to convince me that it could work, because it never does. It's Murphy's Law, kid. Look what happened. You wouldn't have predicted this in a million years."

"So where'd you get the pictures, Leo?"

Leo pulled two business cards from his pocket and read them. "From Special Investigator Raymond Bequette and Detective Donald Reston, IAD."

"I'll bite," she said. 'What's it all about?"

"They'd like to talk to you."

"About *what*?"

"About your relationship with a man who has been under surveillance and under suspicion for dealing dope for more than a year, since before he left Vice Control Division."

"They think he sold me dope? Or that I supplied it? Did they get any pictures of that?"

"If you'd done that, they'd had pictures, you can be sure of that."

"Their pictures tell the whole story of our relationship. They know where we went and how long we stayed there and how many times we went out. That's more than I know. What could I tell them?"

"They don't know, but you spent as much time with him as anyone during the time he was trafficking in drugs. They think you might be able to shed a little light on the subject for them."

"What do you think, Leo? I've told you why I didn't think our relationship was anything you needed to be aware of, and I admit I was breaking the rules, rationalizing, whatever you want to call it. I love my job, and I love working for you, *and* I wanted that and my relationship with Jim. I can see how it's gotten me into bigger trouble, and I'm sorry it cost you your confidence in me. But do you think that I could be aware that Jim was doing what they think he was doing and still keep seeing him? Could I have become aware of his activity and then not told you of my mistake?"

"I can't imagine."

"Thanks for that, anyway."

"You're welcome, but I also can't understand you're being so close to the man for this long and not catching on."

"Catching on to what? Have you considered the possibility that I know the man better than people who shoot pictures with a telephoto lens from a hundred yards away? I'm telling you that Jim Purcell is the farthest thing from a dope dealer I've ever met. He never talked about it. He never used it. He never possessed it. He never ran in those circles. It just isn't true, Leo."

Leo reached back into the same drawer and produced another envelope full of photographs. He scooped up the ones of Jim and Jennifer and replaced them with a couple dozen shots of James Purcell with other people.

Jennifer put a trembling hand up to her mouth, and, as much as she wanted to pull away and run from the room, she couldn't take her eyes off the pictures. Even in dark glasses, Jim was recognizable. Even in shots taken by infrared camera in the dead of night, it was most definitely him.

There were pictures of him in broad daylight, some in uniform, some in clothes she didn't recognize, some with his hair styled differently. But it was him. He was talking with Frank Akeley at a street corner, taking something from Trudy Janus in the parking lot of a shopping center on Western Avenue, in conference with Bill Much somewhere in Uptown, looking around to be sure no one was watching.

There he was with known hoodlums from outside the police department too. The mob-related figure from south of the Loop whom Jennffer had written a story about when he was sentenced in the spring. The gang leader from the West Side ghetto who was up on charges six times before being sent to Stateville Penitentiary in Joliet a few months earlier. The police officer who was fired after being convicted of stealing truckloads of auto tires in a suburban heist.

"You recognize some of these creeps?"

She nodded, shuddering.

"Your boyfriend got too close to the fire one too many times, and IAD got him. You want to see more?"

She didn't, but part of her needed to. She wasn't about to let this thing drop until she had talked to Jim. Love may not have been what she felt for the sad looking creature in the photos, but she did pity him. He surely wouldn't have a friend in the world once all the dirt came out.

So this was what was going to happen to her love if she found he was guilty. It wasn't so much anger and resentment. It was pity. And wonder. And curiosity. When had it started? What caused it? What made him so good at concealing it from even the woman he appeared to love?

Why would he risk his cover by spending time with a police reporter? Did knowing that she had been fooled give him the false sense of security that allowed him to be the subject of so much surveillance without his catching on? Did it ultimately lead to his arrest? Should she take some morbid comfort in that? That she may have been partially responsible for his finally being stopped by providing him a sense of well-being that he shouldn't have had?

She had a feeling the bitterness would return—the bitterness she had felt when she first suspected him. But for now she was stunned. "Let me see the other photos," she said.

"The other material isn't photos. It's documents, affidavits."

She scanned a few. Depositions taken from policemen at lower levels. Civilian dope dealers, some in prison, some still on the street, telling of their contacts within the police department. Some of it dated back many years. Much of it related to the big scandal a year and a half before.

But the parts that related to Jim Purcell went back to just before he had left VCD. That's where it had started. Had he been sincere about his reasons for getting out? She had thought of sexual temptation, maybe financial temptation. She'd never thought of drugs, let alone dealing.

But maybe that was it. He left VCD to clean up his act, to get an assignment—he had hoped in Homicide where drugs were irrelevant. But he got into the wrong precinct. He got in where the big stuff was going on, and he couldn't stay out.

Why was she pitying him? If he had lived a lie for all those months and she had told her father—thumbed his nose at her love, he didn't deserve anything from her.

"What does this all mean for me, Leo?"

"I've been thinking a lot about that, Jenn. I can see you were hoodwinked by this guy, and that makes me feel bad. I never really figured that you knew all this, or I'd have let you go without even talking with you. But that wouldn't have been fair. Now that I've talked to you, I have to lay it out straight.

"I'm suspending you indefinitely for insubordination for not telling me of a relationship that was potentially dangerous for the *Day*. You have no idea what it was like for me today, begging the boys from IAD not to release your name to any other media. They agreed not to, but they couldn't guarantee for how long. They want to talk to you, as I said, but there's no telling what might happen after that.

"So you're off the beat and off the job until this whole police thing is over. That could be a year. And the only way I can let you back is if your guy is acquitted or if your name never gets into it. Now we both know Purcell is as good as up the river. And I've got to tell you that I'd have to wait two years of not seeing your name associated with this thing anywhere before I'd be comfortable in putting you back on the beat."

It was as if he had punched her in the stomach. He hadn't said she was actually fired, but he might as well have. What was she supposed to do for two years? Hibernate? Go to a competitor? With his sense of justice, Leo would tell anyone who called for a reference that they should be careful of her for a while.

Now what? Run home again? He had said IAD wanted to talk to her. He had also said that if he had let her go without even talking to her, it wouldn't have been fair. Was she being fair to Jim? Didn't she owe it to him, if not to herself, to talk to him before she abandoned him?

Her father had said to believe in Jim until he was proven guilty. Neither of them knew how quickly that might happen. But had he meant "proven" guilty, or "found" guilty by a court? Was she grasping at straws? Perhaps. But she decided she would do everything in her power to follow her father's advice, at least until she talked to Jim. IAD first, then Jim.

"I understand, Leo," she said lifelessly. "Are you going to be able to keep this out of the *Day*, I mean with Bobby knowing?"

"Bobby knows?"

She nodded.

"You told Bobby, but you didn't tell me?"

"*I* didn't tell him, Leo. I thought *he* told *you!*"

"He never told me anything, the little—" He caught himself. "Ah, anyway, I'll deal with him. I'm sorry, Jenny. I'm going to miss you. I loved you liked a sister. A daughter anyway."

His calling her Jenny grated on her, and she almost asked him not to ever call her that again. But then she realized that she likely wouldn't have to worry about it.

Nine

Jennifer appeared upset enough as she cleaned out her desk that no one had the courage to ask what was going on. It was apparent she was leaving, and not just for a few days. They'd have to find out from Leo.

One of her messages was from Donald Reston of the IAD. It said she could locate him the next afternoon at the Numbers Racket Club on Dearborn. Jennifer was grateful that she didn't have to talk to him right away.

She went home and tried to sort things out. Jennifer knew she was tired, but she just couldn't sleep. Most of the night she sat by the window, staring into the dark talking to herself and thinking and praying.

She realized how bone weary she was the next day when she stepped from her car on Dearborn. Money for this meter would not be reimbursed by the *Day*. It was a good thing Scott had left her some money. More than half of it had been spent on the funeral and the cost of settling his modest estate, but there was enough left to live on for a while if necessary. But probably not enough to last long if she used any of it to bail Jim Purcell out of jail.

I must be tired, she thought. *Still thinking about getting him out after seeing those pictures Leo has. What's the matter with me?* She decided she was so enamored of her own father that she had been somehow catapulted into a benefit-of-the-doubt-giving posture that couldn't be shaken, even by condemning pictures and affidavits.

There was something about the whole ordeal that still didn't sit well with her, but she couldn't put her finger on it. It wasn't that she thought she was above being conned. Nor that Jim would have been incapable of it. But she thought she had glimpsed the core of the man. And what she had seen in Jim was not what she'd seen in the photographs. Oh, those were pictures of him, all right. But if she had to choose between the two personas, she'd choose the one she knew, not just because that was the way she wanted it or because that would make it all pleasant, but because she really felt—down deep—that she knew the real Jim Purcell. And she loved him.

Did she, could she, love him if the Jim in the pictures was the real character? No, she decided. She couldn't. She wouldn't be reacting this way if she knew for sure that he was guilty. But she didn't know if she was reacting this way because she wasn't convinced of his guilt, or if she wasn't convinced of his guilt because of the way she was reacting. That would sound crazy to a person like Don Reston. It even sounded crazy to Jennifer.

She asked for Reston at the counter and was directed to racquetball court number three. She watched from the cutout in the wall upstairs and tried to guess which player was Reston. Not knowing the game, it was hard for Jennifer to tell who was winning or what was going on. But the most agile, the most in-shape player was a tall, almost gangly, dark-haired man in red shorts and a blue cutoff sweatshirt. He was playing barefoot, which she didn't understand either.

Decked out in a jogger's ensemble was an older man, probably mid-forties, who was paunchy, sweated a lot, and was always stopping to catch his breath. He was an all right player, she guessed. But the taller man dominated. He started each play, when he was in control of the ball, by bouncing it very lightly on the floor so that it rose only a few inches, and then he didn't hit it until it was on its way down again.

The taller man stepped and twisted his whole body and drove his racket into the ball with such force that it slammed off the front wall and came hurtling at the ankles of his opponent, usually causing him to dance just to get his racket on it.

Jennifer folded her coat neatly over her arm and leaned against the ledge. She watched and thought for several minutes, guessing the taller man was Reston. Suddenly the other man lost his balance while stepping into a low shot close to the front wall. As she watched him tumble to the floor, she nearly missed seeing the ball career off the wall and head straight at her. As she dropped out of sight, she saw the tall man whirl to follow the flight of the ball.

"A little help, please," he called.

She ran after the ball and retrieved it just before it would have bounced down the carpeted stairway. Embarrassed, she tossed it through the opening again without showing her face. But when she didn't hear the game begin again, she cautiously peered down.

Both men were looking at her. They smiled and looked at each other. "It's her," the older one said.

"Jennifer Grey?" asked the younger.

She nodded.

"Can you give me a minute to polish off this turkey, and we'll be right with you?"

She'd been right. It was Reston. When they'd finished, he hollered back up at her. "We'll grab a shower, then we can talk right here, if that's all right with you."

They looked both tired and refreshed later in casual clothes as they sat across from her in overstuffed chairs in the upstairs lounge. She found herself strangely nervous, though she'd interviewed cops hundreds of times.

"I'm Don Reston; call me Don. This is Ray Bequette; call him Gramps." The men laughed. Jennifer tried to.

"Let's get right to the point, Miss Grey."

"Mrs."

"Oh, I'm sorry. I guess we just figured—"

"You figured that since I'm dating, I couldn't be a widow."

"I'm sorry, ma'am; I was unaware of that. Your boss told you by now, no doubt, that the Internal Affairs Division has been observing you and Officer Purcell for many months. Were you totally unaware of his involvement in the drug scene?"

"I still am."

"I beg your pardon?"

"I still am totally unaware of his involvement in the drug scene."

"I was under the impression that Mr. Stanton was to show you some of the results of our surveillance."

"I saw your photographs and your affidavits."

"Then you can't really say you are completely in the dark about our suspicions of Purcell."

"Fair enough. I know what you think about him, and I know what people have said about him. But I never had an inkling about this, and I'm not ready to accept it."

"What more will it take to convince you?"

"I need to talk to him, of course."

"We can arrange that."

"You can?"

"Certainly."

"What's in it for you?"

"We need a little information. We thought you might be willing to help us get it."

"You mean trying to get something out of him that I would then pass along to you? You've got to be kidding. I couldn't do that."

"You're above that?"

"I'm not an undercover cop. Maybe if I were I'd throw my scruples to the wind."

"Your boss told us he thought you were in the dark about Purcell until now too."

"He was right. Can you tell me something? How much of your information did you get from my assistant at the *Day?*"

The two looked at each other. "I didn't even know you had an assistant until I heard from your boss. Stanton called this morning and told me that he had reprimanded your assistant because he knew about you and Purcell and never said a word to Stanton about it. Stanton figured he was trying to set you up so he could have your job."

Jennifer sat back and stared at the wall.

"Do you mind if we get back to your boyfriend?"

"You mean back to the dirty work you just asked me to do?"

"Purcell betrayed you."

"Possibly."

"You wouldn't like to return the favor?"

Jennifer removed her coat from her lap and draped it on a nearby chair. She looked first at Reston, then at Bequette. "Maybe if I really thought he was guilty, I could justify this."

"How are you going to find out?"

"I'm going to ask him. To the best of my knowledge, he has never lied to me. He's answered everything I've ever asked him. I know him well, I think. If he's doing a number on me, I'll know when I ask him straight out."

"And if you determine that he is what we think he is?"

"I'll be disappointed, of course."

"Of course. But will you tell us what he says?"

"I'll think about it."

"We can only arrange a meeting for you if you agree to give us information afterward."

"And what if I become convinced during our conversation that he is innocent?"

Reston and Bequette looked at each other. Reston shrugged. Bequette took over in a fatherly manner. "Mrs. Grey, I hate to tell you, but apparently you're not getting our drift. The man is guilty. There is no doubt about that. We have enough evidence to put him away for years. We don't want information from you that will incriminate him. We simply want all we can get from him in the event that he doesn't turn state's witness. Frankly, this move of his not to seek counsel was a crafty thing to do, and it makes us nervous. Whatever he was trying to accomplish with it, it worked. We don't know what he's up to, but apparently he's stalling for some reason.

"It could be he's worried about some of his key contacts, worried that they'll try to harm him now that he's been burned. That's a good reason to stay in jail. Maybe someone else is clearing out of town while he's stalling us. This is our last case with IAD, and we'd like to clean the thing up right, wouldn't you?"

"I have no problem with what you're trying to do. It's just that I would have to be totally convinced that Jim's guilty before I could ever cooperate with you in trying to implicate other people by getting information out of him."

Bequette turned to Reston and talked quietly, though not trying to keep Jennifer from hearing. "Don, I frankly don't think the man will try to maintain his innocence any longer. He hasn't announced how he'll plead, but he's got to know what we've got on him. If she goes in there under the assumption that he's guilty and that the sham is over, my guess is he'd give it up and would try to determine if Mrs. Grey here would stick by him or throw him over. If he does that—and we might be able to help that happen by getting him special permission to talk with her longer in a more casual setting than the interview cells then she'll know, and, if I'm reading her right, she'll help us out all she can."

Reston looked to Jennifer. She tilted her head and pursed her lips as if to say, "I suppose." What she did say was, "Well, if Jim tells me he's guilty, I can't argue with that, can I?"

"I don't see how he can say otherwise," Bequette said. "I've been concentrating on Bill Much for several months, but of course I've helped Don tail Purcell at times too. We've all worked together on this case, each specializing on one of the four and helping out with the others."

"Jim was your mark?" Jennifer asked Reston.

"Yes, ma'am. I'd been seeing a lot of you two together lately."

"Yeah, well, I'm not too thrilled about that. But tell me, what did you see Jim do?"

"With you?"

"No, I know that. What your camera saw was all there was to see."

"That's what we thought. You never spent time with him at his place or yours, did you?"

"I've never even been in his place."

Reston shook his head in wonder. "So anyway, you were asking?"

"What you saw Jim do while you were tailing him all this time. I didn't see your name in the affidavits, did I?"

"No, my deposition and testimony will come nearer the time of the trials. It takes us weeks to prepare our presentations, and of course, each of us will talk about what we saw all four suspects doing."

"And what I give you—if I do—from my talk with Jim—will go into your testimony?"

"Absolutely."

"Then I'd better be sure he's guilty. And that he willfully betrayed me. And that I'm up to this kind of revenge."

"I don't think you should call it revenge," Reston said. "It's the civic duty of any law abiding citizen."

"That's a little idealistic after what I've been through with Jim the past several months," she said.

"I've been through a few things with him too," Reston said.

"Are you going to give me some examples?"

"What do you want to hear?"

Jennifer was growing impatient. "Anything. Something solid. Something incriminating. Something that will convince me the way you're convinced."

Reston stood and walked to the iron railing that overlooked the first floor. Joggers were padding past. He put both hands on the rail and hung his head low to his chest. He turned and came back, sitting right next to Jennifer, which startled her. His dark eyes looked weary.

"Let me tell you something," he said. "I don't much like the job I've had to do the last couple of years. I don't like spying on cops, even bad ones. I don't get any big kick out of building a case against someone and knowing it's going to ruin him forever. I know these guys deserve it, and I know that ruining them for life is the price we pay to get them off the street— and getting them off the street is something I have no qualms about because we deal with the results of dope addiction in nearly every case we handle, week in and week out.

"And when that surveillance work is over, like it is now, the toughest part of the process begins. We take our notes and our photos and our tape recordings, and we start a written case against someone, a case that is so airtight that we never have to worry that our work has been in vain.

"I could sit here and tell you stories about James Purcell that would take me all night. Places I've seen him, people I've seen him with, marked money I've seen him take, dope I've checked in that he's sold to undercover narcs. You want just one incident? I wouldn't know where to start.

"There's something we don't do, Mrs. Grey. We don't arrest them and then see them on the street again. When IAD has busted a guy, he stays busted. Because we wouldn't even go to the trouble of the dangerous arrest of an armed man unless we had him so dead to rights that we didn't have to worry that he was going to get away with something.

"My boss, one of the best in the business, is probably never going to wake up again, never see his wife and his daughters again, never be a great example to young cops again because your boyfriend's boss tried to kill him. A cop shot a cop, and don't let anybody ever tell you that Frank Akeley didn't know who he was firing on Tuesday morning."

Reston had grown emotional, and Bequette looked concerned. Jennifer's last vestiges of hope were fleeting. He sounded so sure. He ought to be sure. He was sure.

"I put the responsibility for the shooting of John Lucas right in the laps of every one of the big four in the Sixteenth Precinct. Every one of 'em ought to get the chair if he dies, because they all had a hand in it. They were the reason he was on the street that night, doing a job that a lesser boss wouldn't have done.

"So you see why I don't want to talk about the specifics in the James Purcell case? You see why these guys, all of them, make me sick when I think about them? You'll get your specifics. They'll all come out in the trial, and they'll be in every paper in town."

Jennifer was sorry she had asked. She couldn't speak, but she tried to tell him with her expression that she at least understood what he was trying to say.

Bequette broke the tension. "You still want to see Purcell?"

She nodded.

"All right. We'll set it up. You'll get a call. Probably from Purcell himself; he hasn't used his call yet. And you'll be able to talk to him in the anteroom downtown. You'll be searched and will be allowed to take nothing in or out with you. But we'll give you all the time you need."

"When?"

"Tomorrow morning at nine."

Ten

The next morning Jennifer dressed as if she were going on the most important date of her life. She was, of course. But the mirror told the story of the night before. She had been in bed twelve hours, yet she did more praying than sleeping, more thinking than dreaming.

She tried covering the dark circles under her eyes with makeup, but that backfired. She decided she looked like a raccoon and hoped that Jim would think her clothes were so nice he wouldn't notice her face.

Why am I thinking about trivia anyway? she chided herself. How I look will be the last thing on his mind and on mine if I can keep my thoughts straight.

She had settled it, she decided in her car. If Jim was guilty—and she would know either by his not trying to hide it anymore or by seeing through him if he did—she felt no responsibility for his actions or for protecting him. She would lose whatever it was she felt for him, and she would feel no compulsion to keep from IAD anything he might say incriminating anyone else.

It was when she reached police headquarters downtown that she realized she had never received a confirming call—not from Jim, not from IAD, not from anyone. Should she wait until she saw Bequette or Reston? Or should she just go in and see if she was expected? There were plenty of unmarked squad cars, but how would she know if any of them belonged to men from IAD?

"I would like to see a prisoner," she told the sergeant at the desk.

"Name?"

"Officer James Purcell."

"No! Your name!"

"Jennifer Grey."

"Press is not allowed to see prisoners, especially that one."

"I'm not here as press, Sergeant. I have been cleared to talk with Officer Purcell."

"You got papers?"

"No, I assumed you would have received something."

"I got nothing."

"Well, could you please check? It was cleared through IAD and—"

"IAD don't cut any ice around here, lady. I run the jail."

"But wouldn't you have clearance papers for certain visitors?"

"Lemme look," he said, disgusted. He rummaged around on his desk and came up with a yellow carbon copy of something. "Well, whadya know?" She edged closer.

"You're to see Purcell at nine o'clock in the anteroom. It's all set."

"Thank you."

"Except—"

"Except?"

"Except it ain't nine o'clock yet, is it? I got to make sure I got personnel that'll allow you to be in the anteroom."

"I was told there would be no one else in there but us."

"Yeah, so I gotta have men outside the windows and outside the door, don't I?"

"How long will that take? It's ten to nine."

"I don't know. I'll let you know when the room and the prisoner are ready for you, Miss Grey."

"Mrs."

"Whatever."

Jennifer sat on a wood bench for nearly forty minutes, doing everything in her power to avoid asking what was taking so long. Every time she would come to the end of her patience and start to move toward the sergeant again, he would hold up a hand and mouth silently, "I will let you know."

Crazy ideas floated through her head. Jim was a drug addict. A schizophrenic. He would cry and beg her to forgive him. He would deny it, but she would see through him. He had been moved to another facility. He had finally hired a lawyer and was out on bond. He had tried to escape. He had been caught. He had escaped.

"Miss Grey!"

Mrs., Jennifer thought as she jumped up and ran over to the sergeant, but she said nothing.

"The prisoner has declined the conference," the man said.

"What?"

"He don't wanna see anybody."

"Does he know who's here to see him?"

"Yes, ma'am, if you want it like that, he don't wanna see you."

Jennifer spun in a circle, confused. What was she supposed to make of this? Didn't he realize that until he got a lawyer, she was probably the only friend he had? She had held out hope—she still did—and she shouldn't have after all she'd heard. Something was still unresolved. Something he didn't know but should have. He needed to know that she loved him. That was really why she was here. Guilty or not, a future for them or not, whether she loved him when she knew the whole truth or not, he needed to know that she loved the man she knew. She had to tell him.

She hadn't been gone from her job long enough to lose her ingenuity. "Can you get a message to him?"

"I could if I wanted to. I tol' ya I run the jail. But I don't wanna. Bye-bye."

"Maybe this message is as much for you as it is for him then. How would you like me to make a scene, right here in the lobby? How would you like it to appear in every paper in town that the former police reporter for the *Chicago Day* couldn't get in to see a prisoner and that she caused such a ruckus she had to be thrown out?"

"That I don't need. I'm in enough trouble as it is with all the baloney that goes on *inside* the bars. That'd be great; a fruitcake *outside* the bars goes nuts."

"That's what you're going to have to answer for."

"Awright, what's the message?"

"Just that. I'll make a scene that'll embarrass him and you if he won't see me."

"He'll see ya. Wait in the anteroom."

Jennifer couldn't believe herself. *I've gone from a halfway intelligent police reporter to a conniving, unemployed, boisterous, lovesick woman in two days!*

She sat at the end of a long gray table, wondering what she should do when he entered. Embrace him? Smile at him? Tear into him verbally? The door opened, and a matron came in. Jennifer was searched, and her handbag and coat and jewelry were taken. She sat back down but hadn't even had time to collect herself when Jim walked in. Her heart raced. She stood, but he sat at the other end of the table. She felt foolish standing there and sat back down.

He looked like his old self except that he was wearing city-issue blue denims. He still had that shy look, that gentle air. She didn't know what she had expected. A monster? A shouter? A hard-looking criminal?

"How are you?" she said, her voice quavering.

He ignored the question. "I'm sorry I said I didn't want to see you, Jennifer. But it's just that the timing isn't right. I didn't want you to see me in here like this. I know you've been around these places, but you don't like seeing me in this get-up, do you?"

"That's not the reason you didn't want to see me," she tried weakly, fighting tears. "If I didn't see you here, where was I ever going to see you?"

"You could have seen me later. Soon."

"Where?"

"Jennifer, the truth is there's something going on here that you know nothing about. I never told you anything about it because I simply couldn't. You don't understand it, and you won't be able to understand it until I'm able to tell you all about it."

"I'm afraid I do know about it, Jim. I know more than I want to know. I can't believe you could have kept it from me all this time. I feel so stupid, so used. Betrayed."

"But you understand why I couldn't talk about it, don't you?"

"No! Did you think I wouldn't understand?"

"Would you have?"

She bit her lip and stood, walking to the window where she saw three uniformed guards kibbitzing. "I don't understand how you could do this to me."

"Jenn, there was no other way. If I had told you, it would have spoiled everything. I couldn't take the chance."

"You don't think everything's spoiled now?"

"All we have right now is a timing problem, Jennifer."

"You think time will heal this wound?"

"Jennifer, I'm gratified to hear that you miss me, and I miss you too, but this is temporary, and—"

"It goes much deeper than missing you, Jim. I love you. I need you. And now I'm so disappointed in you that I don't know what to think."

Jim stared at her, his eyes narrowing. She pressed her lips together to keep from crying. "There, you see?" she said, scolding him. "I love you in spite of this, and I had decided not to!"

He stood and moved toward her, but she turned her back to him. "Jennifer. You're disappointed in me? You love me in spite of this? In spite of what?"

"What have we just been talking about Jim? I know all about it! I've seen the pictures! I've read the reports! I've talked with the people from IAD! What are you going to do, deny it all now? What have you been saying about my not understanding what you couldn't tell me, if you're claiming now that you don't see what's come between us?"

He turned and rested both palms on the table, leaning over from the waist. Then he stood up and drew his palms to his face and slid them slowly down his cheeks. He let out a short sigh of surprise and whispered, "You believe I've really been busted!"

Jennifer was speechless. Her mouth fell open, and she just turned to stare at him. He looked at her without turning his head and grinned. "Jennifer! You don't really think—no, you—oh, Jenn, I'm sorry. You couldn't have thought—"

"Jim, what are you saying?"

"You said you talked to the guys at IAD? Who'd you talk to?"

"Don Reston and Ray somebody."

"Bequette?"

"Yes."

"And they didn't tell you?"

"They told me everything, Jim, and you're in a lot of trouble."

"They're not telling you the truth because you're a reporter," he guessed, but his smile had frozen. He'd lost his edge, his confidence. Jennifer read the worst into it.

"I'm not a reporter anymore, Jim. I lost my job because of you. And it would be worth it if I knew it had all been a big mistake."

"You lost your job? Well, it was no mistake, Jenn. But I'm not supposed to tell you about it yet, that's all. Someone will be bailing me out soon—in fact they should have already—and then the whole story will come out."

Jennifer sat down. "Jim, if you're trying to tell me that you were in on this from IAD's side, I've got to tell you, I don't believe it. I don't know who's trying to con who, but they showed me some stuff that makes you look pretty bad."

Jim's confusion and fear showed. "Why would they show you that stuff? Did they know you'd lost your job?"

"They wanted me to pump you for information on other people who might be incriminated in the case. They showed the stuff to my boss too, and to the publisher."

"What for, Jenn? What's it all about?"

"They thought I would know all about your dope-dealing because I'd spent so much time with you the past several months. Jim, what is going on?"

"I'm not sure. I'll feel like a fool if I'm supposed to be going along with this and then I tell you everything at the drop of a hat. Maybe it's a test. Maybe I shouldn't have told you anything, but just played along, pretended I'd been caught. But I can't do that to you, Jenn. I never thought you'd really think I'd been busted. But since you did, I probably should have let you go on thinking it until this thing blew over."

"If you think this thing is going to blow over, you'd better talk to Don Reston. He was nearly in tears today, telling me that he holds you and Much and Janus every bit as responsible for Lucas's death as Akeley."

"Lucas died?" Jim said, almost shouting.

"No, I didn't mean that; he was saying if Lucas died."

"Reston's a good actor. Could he have been bluffing you?"

"For what reason? Anyway, I don't think so. He'd have had to be a better con man than you are."

"Jenn, I want to tell you the whole story, but I have to make sure I'm not messing up the operation. We've been on this one for too long."

"You lost me a long time ago."

"You never told me you loved me before."

"Jim, how can you change the subject like that?"

"I love you too, you know."

"Don't do this to me, Jim. I can't make it compute."

"I couldn't tell you I loved you before because I knew we were being watched and photographed, and I didn't want you to be embarrassed by anything we did."

"You knew we were being photographed? And you knew by whom?"

"Of course."

"I've got to tell you something, Jim. If you think you have friends in IAD, you don't. Either those men I talked to today think you're as guilty as you look, or I am the worst judge of character who ever walked the earth."

"You're serious."

"You bet I am."

"All right, Jennifer. I'm going to tell you what's been going on, but you can't tell anyone. If you love me, you'll protect my confidence."

"Jim, don't put that on me, please! I've got all this evidence on one side showing that you've been living a lie in front of me for months, and I've got you on the other, telling me not to tell the people who sent me here that you told me anything. I came here under the condition that I would tell them what you said. You think you're breaking confidences; how do you like that one?"

"I don't know what to think, Jenn, but you're going to have to hear me out on this. I may be the worst undercover cop Chicago's ever had, but I don't know what else to do with a woman who says she loves me."

Jennifer hid her face in her hands. She wanted whatever she was about to hear to be true. She raised her head and looked Jim full in the face as if to say, "I'm listening. Pour it on."

Eleven

"When I first requested a transfer from Vice Control Division, I got in hot water from my captain."

"Why did you want to transfer?"

"I already told you that, Jenn. I may have kept a lot from you, but I never lied to you, OK?"

"OK, so you quit VCD because you had a hard time reconciling it with your faith."

"Exactly. And I took a lot of heat for that inside the department, especially from my boss and his boss. They sent memos around, even up to the commissioner, trying to head off this precedent of people deciding they didn't like their assignments and all that."

"Yes, and it was in all the papers."

"Right, but that was by design."

"Meaning?"

"It was staged, planned, set up. You know, Jenn, that you never got anything the police department didn't want you to have, and you never missed something they wanted you to cover. You may not have run with what they gave you, but they tried anyway."

"I don't follow."

"They're news manipulators. And they're good at it. I know from having spent enough time with you that you would not agree with tactics like that, but I think in some instances they have their place. It's debatable. That's why I thought Bequette and Reston were setting you up. But if they went to your boss and higher and showed them all the stuff, well I may have a serious problem—one that depends a lot on the health of John Lucas."

"You think they could indict all of you in connection with his death?"

"No, you're still not getting it, are you?"

"No, but I'm trying. Keep going."

"Anyway, the word inside the department was that I was some kind of a goody-goody, and there was a lot of speculation about whether they'd make a scapegoat of me so other guys wouldn't try the same thing with their assignments. Of course, most of them want Vice Control duty. They get a charge out of it.

"Well, right about that time, I got contacted by John Lucas. He said he liked my attitude and that he had gotten permission to consider me for IAD. He wanted to do some checking and interview me for several days. We met at various places and talked for hours. The one thing he told me never to forget was that a good internal affairs man has to keep secrets even from himself."

"What did he mean by that?"

"It was an exaggeration to make a point. Most people can't keep a secret for half a day. Internal Affairs tests their guys all the time, starting rumors and seeing where they lead, how long it takes the story to get distorted and come back, and all that. Confidentiality was a major prerequisite. But it wasn't as important as an unimpeachable record.

"Lucas had checked me out and decided I was the type of person he wanted in IAD. He set it up with the commissioner for me to appear to suffer for my request of a change of assignment, and people within and without the department bought it. The people in the Sixteenth thought they were really getting me and doing the commissioner a favor by giving me the dog assignments, the night desk and then the Officer Friendly thing. It couldn't have been more perfect for what I was really assigned to do.

"Lucas gave me a couple of drug-related assignments in VCD before I was transferred. He gave me the dope and the money, and he had his men check me out. He was pleased when they reported back that I was somebody they could nail and that they should keep an eye on me.

"My point is this, Jennifer. For the past year or so, I have ultimately reported to John Lucas. We hardly ever saw each other because he had not even told his own men. And he trained them to stay on my tail. That made it nearly impossible for me to ever meet with him."

"When was he going to tell his men?"

"He wasn't sure. He said he thought he might not tell them until the night of the big four arrests. You know, when Reston busted me that night, I only played along for the sake of the uniformed men with him. But I wondered if he had been told yet because he played it so straight. No winks, no jokes, no anything."

"Well, Jim, someone else had to know. Even if Lucas decided not to tell anyone until after you were in jail, his secretary had to know, didn't she? And who checked you out for him in the first place?"

"That was just it. He did most of the checking himself, and then he assigned the ones who had checked me out first to tail me a while. After the first few drug sales in VCD, they were all convinced I was bad. Lucas told me he was getting a real kick out of having his own inside guy that no one else knew about. He didn't think it was too dangerous because it was only temporary, and his real reason was to give him a fail-safe look at his own team. They did well."

"They did too well, Jim. But the commissioner knows, right?"

"The commissioner *should* know. Lucas reports directly and confidentially to him. Has to. That's the only way Internal Affairs can work."

Jennifer leaned back in her chair and studied James Purcell's eyes. "An undercover undercover undercover man. If I didn't want to believe it so badly, I probably wouldn't."

He smiled. "Lucas called me that once, not in those words. Said I was his triple threat. When the undercover guys investigating the undercover guys are not worthy, he's got one more ace up his sleeve."

"Jim, do you think Bequette and Reston were putting me on today and that they really know?"

"If I thought that, I'd have played along with *them*. Sorry to have to tell you that, but it has been my job for more than a year. Their talking to you and your boss and everybody and costing you your job, that's what scares me. Reston becoming emotional is nothing new. He's sincere, but he can playact that bit as well as anyone I've ever seen."

"What do we do about them?"

"I don't worry about them unless something happens to Lucas."

"Something could have already happened to Lucas, Jim. He's that bad."

Purcell stood and paced. "You want to help?"

"Why do you think I'm here?"

"To help the people who think I'm guilty, isn't that what you said?"

"I was confused. Of course I want to help. I believe you, Jim."

He stepped behind where she sat and put his hands on her shoulders. "That's the second-nicest thing you've said to me today," he said. "Anyway, I think you'd better get to Lucas's secretary and Eric O'Neill, he's the one who busted—"

"Janus. I know. I covered this story, remember?"

"Hey, if you clear me, will you get your job back?"

"I guess. Somehow that seems insignificant right now. Anyway, I'll go and see anyone you say. Who else?"

"Well, you could talk to the commissioner, but let's save him as a last resort. If you don't get anywhere with the guys from IAD, send Reston and Bequette to see me. I'll see what I can do. Maybe there's something I can tell them about Lucas, some inside joke, some special name he has for them, something that will convince them that I work for the man too."

Jennifer smiled for the first time since she had chatted with her father. "It's nice to have a job to do," she said. "I'm sorry I doubted you, Jim, but it was all so—"

"I know. Listen, you were looking at dirt dug up by the Chicago PD IAD, and they're the best in the business. If I saw all they had on me, I might doubt me too. Listen, Jenn, if you don't mind, find out what you can as soon as you can, because if these guys are serious and Lucas doesn't pull through, I might as well be guilty, because I won't have a chance."

"I'll do everything I can; you know I will. I'll be praying for you."

"You know who I'll be praying for?"

"Who?"

"Lucas."

Jennifer stood and found herself face to face with Jim Purcell, the man she realized she would have loved in spite of herself, in spite of himself, and in the middle of the most confusing time of her life. They held each other for several minutes, her face buried in his shoulder. And she cried.

Perhaps she had not done as well as her father might have hoped in her attempt to give Jim the benefit of the doubt. But now there was no longer any doubt, and she could think of no greater joy.

She drove to her apartment and bounded up the steps, wanting to laugh and cry and sing and scream all at the same time. She was reminded of her seventh birthday when her father gave her her first bicycle. He had sent her to the garage on an errand, and she had seen that beautiful bike with a big blue bow and a card with her name on it, and she ran back in tears to thank him before she even touched it. What a gift that had been. And what a gift this had been.

When she lost Scott, there was no bringing him back. She prayed that it had all been a bad dream, but it wasn't, and she knew it would always hurt. But now she had Jim. She would not let this love be snatched away, not if she had anything to say about it. And the beauty was, she had everything to say about it.

She called Don Reston and asked him to meet her as soon as possible. They met at a coffee shop on LaSalle Drive. She happily, earnestly spilled the story. "So if you were trying to get to me through him for some reason, it didn't work because it scared him. You can be straight with me now if you know that he's working with IAD too."

Reston stared at her sullenly. "I'm sorry, Mrs. Grey, but I think you're a victim of a vivid imagination."

"I'm not imagining anything. I talked to him, just like you said, and—"

"I'm talking about his imagination," Reston said. "It's just not true. Lucas would have told us, and believe me, he didn't."

"Would anyone else in IAD know?"

"I'll call Bequette, but I'm afraid you're in for a big disappointment. I'm not happy that you blew our assignment either, because if you had just told him you knew he was guilty—"

"I *did!* But he told me everything."

Reston shook his head sadly. "This is no game, ma'am. I'd have no reason to continue any ruse if what you were saying was true. But it's not. Let me call Ray."

He slid out of the booth, and she called after him, "See if you can get ahold of Mr. O'Neill for me too. Someone had to know about this."

He nodded and was on the phone for several minutes. Jennifer looked at her watch, wondering if she could squeeze in a meeting with John Lucas's secretary before she left for lunch. She was nervous. Her foot tapped, fingers on both hands drummed the table, her eyes darted all around the room. She was on a mission she had planned to enjoy, but she didn't need any more negative reactions.

Reston returned. He looked glum. "Listen," Jennifer said, "why don't you and Bequette visit Jim and talk to him yourselves?"

"We'd never get permission for something like that. It could spoil everything we're preparing for the trial. I'd really like Purcell's story to be true, for your sake. But I saw what I saw. I suppose it's possible that James Purcell was doing that stuff as part of a bigger setup. But I'm afraid unless John Lucas himself says so, I'd never be able to even admit the longshot possibility of it to anybody but you."

"What did Mr. Bequette say?"

"His reaction was the same as mine. I tried to hit him with it before betraying my own feelings on it, just to be fair to you. He says he heard rumors years ago that Lucas liked to do this sort of thing once in a great while, but never for this long or with stakes this high. You can forget about meeting with O'Neill too. He was with Bequette. You don't want to know what he thought of your idea."

"Yes I do."

"He called it a million-to-one shot."

Jennifer accepted the odds and headed to John Lucas's office where she waited until noon to see Gladys Balderson, the chief's secretary. She was a fussy, precise little woman—friendly, yet formal.

"No, Mrs. Grey," she said sweetly. "I never heard Mr. Lucas mention the name Purcell. But then much of his affairs were private, even from me. He has a file that I do not have a key to, but that is always off limits and has, in fact, in light of the shooting, been impounded."

"How would I gain access to it? It must have Jim's name in it somewhere, even if only his initials in a meeting schedule or something. Surely Mr. Lucas couldn't have kept all his clandestine meetings in his head."

"Surely you don't know Mr. Lucas. I would have thought you might have run into him in your work."

"I've never talked with the man."

"I'm sorry, you asked about access to his private file. I believe only a municipal judge or the commissioner of police could grant that, and I would find it highly unlikely in light of your occupation."

Jennifer didn't bother setting her straight about her current employment situation. She was running out of options. "I know it's a long shot," she said, "but I wouldn't forgive myself if I didn't at least try the commissioner. Could I impose on what must be your close relationship with his secretary, your both being at the executive secretarial level and all, and see if you can get me in to see him just for a moment this afternoon?"

"What would you want him to do, honey, open the file for you? I'm sure he wouldn't. Probably couldn't."

"Perhaps he could look for me. I wouldn't have to see anything. I'd just like to see if there's anything at all in that file that would indicate that Mr. Lucas was working with Jim."

"Well, it's a possibility," Miss Balderson said. "I'll call Joan and see." While dialing, she said, "Did you hear that Mr. Lucas rallied this morning?"

"No! Really? Tell me!"

"He apparently gained consciousness early this morning, and the doctors asked the family to join him. One moment."

While Lucas's secretary was talking with the commissioner's secretary, Jennifer prayed that God would spare the man's life. Even as she prayed it, she knew it was selfish. She couldn't care as much for a man she had never spoken with as she did about Jim, whom she loved.

"Tell me your man's full name again, dear," Miss Balderson said, holding a hand over the mouthpiece."

"Officer James Purcell."

When Gladys hung up she said, "You're in luck. The commissioner's secretary took all the information and will check it out herself. She is recording the contents of the entire file verbatim, and if she sees his initials or his name or anything remotely connected with him, if the commissioner approves, she will let you know this afternoon when you arrive for your appointment. Three o'clock. She even remembered that he is Officer Friendly, and she will look up his badge number to see if Mr. Lucas referred to him by that."

"Oh, that's too kind," Jennifer said.

"I don't mind telling you I'm jealous."

"I'm sorry?"

"The man's secret file ought to be handled by his own secretary, wouldn't you think?"

Twelve

Police Commissioner Joseph Masek appeared ill at ease with Jennifer. He began the conversation with a scowl. "You're with the *Day*, aren't you?"

Jennifer spent several minutes explaining why she was no longer with the *Day*. "I see," he said slowly, pressing his fingertips together and staring at her as he leaned back in his chair.

"I can understand your concern," he said. "Yes, I *do* remember the request from Chief Lucas to investigate the young man who wanted out of Vice Control Division. I believe he thought Purcell would be the kind of guy who might make it in IAD. Frankly, my fear at the time, and I expressed it forcefully to John, was that I thought Purcell might look too much like an IAD candidate. He had that fresh-scrubbed look, you know well, of course you know, don't you? Regardless, John felt he would like to check the man out and then bring him in very gradually, test him a little, that sort of thing. I approved that, but then, of course, I removed myself from the situation."

"You removed yourself?"

"Yes. I'm very big on letting the individual chiefs run their respective areas. Of course, in this case, John was requesting permission to maneuver between departments, so he came to me. Now, as a rule, all of John's activity is interdepartmental, and he doesn't need permission when he is investigating any untoward conduct, even within this office."

"Your office?"

"Absolutely. It's the only way an IAD can work properly. He has my full backing and cooperation, and unless he's looking for personnel from another branch, he doesn't get any input from me."

Jennifer took a deep breath. "Well, sir, I just want to assure you that the only reason I'm here is because I'm convinced a huge misunderstanding has occurred, and I didn't know where else to turn."

Commissioner Masek appeared somber. "Mrs. Grey, Officer Purcell is a close personal friend of yours, am I right?"

"Yes."

"I have to tell you that what you have described, John Lucas using a man undercover *within* IAD, is so highly improbable and unusual—though a very, very interesting idea—that I would have to doubt even its remotest possibility."

"Of course it's unusual," Jennifer pleaded, "but that was the only way it could work. Once it comes out, it probably would never work again."

"The point is, I really don't think John would work that way, and he and I go back many, many years. He's been a friend since the early nineteen fifties."

"I didn't know that. You must be very worried."

"I am indeed. My wife and I have been with Sylvia, John's wife, and two or three of the daughters off and on at the hospital ever since yesterday morning. It doesn't look good."

"But I understood he had rallied this morning."

"Well, he gained consciousness for the first time since the shooting, but by the time I arrived there, he was sleeping again. Whether he had lapsed into a coma again, I don't know. But the doctor confided that not a great deal of optimism was justified. John's vital signs are still very weak, very bad."

"May I ask another—"

"I don't hesitate to say," the commissioner continued, staring past Jennifer, "that I am sick in my heart that one police officer would fire on another. It goes much deeper than just the shooting, though, Mrs. Grey. If a younger officer had done it, it might even be easier to take. Then I could say that they don't make cops like they did in my day. But Lucas and I are close to the same age, and Frank Akeley is even older. How does this happen? How does a man with a fine record get mixed up in things like this?"

Jennifer felt sudden compassion for Masek. He was lost in his grief and his fear for the life of his friend. She knew she'd feel the same for Lucas if she spent any time with him. But Lucas was almost an enemy at this point. She constantly pleaded with God to spare his life, knowing all the while that her motive was not as pure as it could be.

She wanted to feel for the man and his wife and his family, but she was thinking of Jim. She admitted silently that she was thinking of herself. Rescuing Jim from this nightmare meant new life for her too.

Commissioner Masek had asked a question to which there was no answer. But he had also interrupted Jennifer's, and she wanted to get back to it.

"Could I ask you a hypothetical question, Commissioner?"

He nodded, still staring past her.

"If John Lucas were to try something innovative as Jim, as Officer Purcell, has suggested, would you have known about it?"

"Not necessarily, no."

"Would it have been likely that you would know?"

"No, I suppose not."

"Then the fact that it sounds so unique to you doesn't really rule out the possibility of it."

He squinted at her. "Are you asking me or telling me?"

"Asking, and I'm sorry if it sounded otherwise."

"That's all right," he said slowly. "Let me tell you something, may I?"

"Please."

"I, uh, have been quite aware of you for some time."

"You have?"

He ignored her. "I am always very interested when a major newspaper puts a new reporter on the police beat. I frankly wasn't sure what I thought of a woman handling the job. That's not to betray any feeling I may or may not have about women in other professions, particularly my own. But I read all three Chicago papers everyday. I care about what they say about law enforcement in this city. And I think you're a good police reporter."

"Thank you."

"That's why I was disappointed when your name came up in this case."

Jennifer held her breath and slowly let it out as he continued.

"Truthfully, I was most disappointed when the top secret documents from John Lucas arrived at my home on Sunday, indicating the names of four officers who would be arrested in the Tuesday morning operation. My heart is always broken when I receive that kind of news.

"It comes in the form of a dossier containing all the essentials on the officer, his record, his years of service, everything. And it culminates in a careful listing—not detailed like it will be for the trial—but a listing of the offenses which have necessitated the arrests.

"Yes, ma'am, I recognized that Officer Purcell was a man John had once considered for work with IAD. But you'd be amazed at how many men who are considered for that kind of work either don't want to do it or aren't qualified. We won't touch a man with *anything* on his record. If he had a tardiness problem when he was a rookie, it's a red flag."

He paused for a long minute. Jennifer didn't know what to make of it. "Are you saying that something in Jim's file disqualified him for IAD?"

"You see, Mrs. Grey, I wouldn't know that. I gave permission for him to be considered, and more than a year later I read a file that contains a very damaging, very horrifying list of offenses against society, against the department, against the law."

"But it was a setup! He was working for Lucas!"

Commissioner Masek leaned forward and rested his chin on his fist, his elbow on the massive desk. He looked into her eyes with a blank expression. She could read nothing. He spoke slowly, carefully. "You have a reason to want to believe that. The only reason I want to believe it is because it saddens me to think that even one patrol officer is involved in the kinds of things in which these four were involved. If for some reason that number could be reduced to three, it would soften the blow for me by just that much. But, Mrs. Grey, the idea of it is preposterous. I'm sorry to have to tell you that. I believe you are sincere; but I'm afraid your young friend is lying to you."

Jennifer started to protest, but he raised a hand to silence her. "Let me put it this way," he tried again. "Let's say I wanted to give you the benefit of the doubt. What could I do? I have no knowledge past what I told you. Yes, I find it ironic that a man who had a tremendous record, a man who was once considered for IAD, was eventually arrested by them. But that is the truth as I know it. And unless someone in IAD tells me otherwise, I have to rely on the arrest documentation. And that looks extremely bad for Officer Purcell."

Jennifer didn't want to cry. She wouldn't. How could this have happened? Was it possible Lucas thought his idea was so novel that he wanted *no one* else to know? Apparently, he had not considered this eventuality. But then no one had.

"Can you tell me anything from Chief Lucas's private file?"

"Yes, but I must first ask you to sign a statement that stipulates that you have been granted access to classified information and that if you ever disseminate it in any fashion, you can be prosecuted."

His secretary dug out the form and brought it in. Jennifer signed quickly as Commissioner Masek scanned the typed list of the contents of Lucas's file. "I'll read you only the pertinent items; I prefer not to show anything to you. The only thing I see here that could have any bearing on Officer Purcell is a list of appointments over the last year with individuals to whom he gives code names: Apollo, Cruiseship, Delta, Eagle;"

Jennifer pressed her fingers to her temples and stared at the floor. "None of them mean anything to me," she said sadly.

"They don't have to mean anything, and probably don't. When we use code names, we use them in categories, that's all. Sometimes it's birds, Robin, Dove, Sparrow, and all the rest. Sometimes it's characters from a classic. John was apparently using names from the space program."

"What if one of the names meant something to Jim?"

"Then we'd have only his word for it, wouldn't we?"

She nodded.

"Anyway," he said, "if I know John, he never would have told any of his contacts his code names for them."

Jennifer stood and reached for Masek's hand. "Thank you for seeing me on such short notice," she said. "Do I have any other recourse? Any at all?"

Masek covered her hand with both of his. "Nothing I can think of," he said. "Unless John Lucas says your man was working for him, Purcell's in a lot of trouble."

Jennifer stepped out of Masek's office just as his secretary was hanging up the phone. *God,* Jennifer prayed silently, *forgive my motive, forgive my selfishness, forgive anything I've done wrong in this whole mess. Just don't let Lucas die.*

His secretary pushed her intercom button. "Mr. Masek?"

"Yes, Joan."

"The hospital just called. Mrs. Lucas is asking for you."

"Mrs. Lucas?"

"Yes, sir. She would like you to come right away, if possible."

"What do I have this afternoon?"

"Sir, it was the doctor, and he said you should hurry."

"Thanks, Joan. Cancel everything. Call the car."

Masek flew out of his office, putting his coat on as he went. Jennifer had to run to keep up with him, a lump rising in her throat. *God, please!*

"Commissioner, may I go with you?"

As he waited for the elevator, he appeared annoyed that she would even ask. He shrugged as if he really didn't know, couldn't decide, and wished she weren't there.

They rode the elevator down together. He still hadn't said no, so she stayed with him. "I won't get in the way." He moved faster now, out the front door to his waiting car. "I want to be there," she said.

Suddenly he stopped and turned on her. "Why?" he demanded angrily. "Whatever for?"

"I don't know!" she said, almost shouting.

He climbed into the backseat and shut the door, leaving her standing there holding her coat, shivering and fighting tears. She was paralyzed, wondering if she should run around the building to her car and race to the hospital on her own. But she'd never get close to Lucas's room if she wasn't with the commissioner.

She clenched her fists and hung her head, then heard the commissioner's car stop at the corner and back up. It screeched to a stop in front of her, and the back door flew open. She didn't hesitate.

When Masek and Jennifer stepped off the elevator in the intensive care unit, they saw the Lucas family standing in a waiting area at the end of the hall, embracing each other and crying.

An emergency team with a crash cart was slowly leaving one of the rooms, and the commissioner and Jennifer knew. Lucas had died.

"No," Masek moaned as he walked slowly toward the family. Jennifer's arms hung straight at her sides, and she forced herself to keep moving on her rubbery legs. Her breath came in short gasps.

Sylvia Lucas noticed Masek and fell into his arms, sobbing loudly and holding him tight. "Oh, Joe, Joe," she said. "Thank you for coming!"

"I'm so sorry, Syl," he said, his long arms wrapped around her.

"He was awake, Joe. He was awake when they called you. He talked."

"He talked?"

"Yeah, Joe. Didn't make any sense, but he tried to talk to me."

Jennifer stepped closer, her heart racing.

"That's nice, Syl," Masek said. "He was tryin' to say good-bye to you; you know that."

"I don't know, Joe," she said, trying to gain control of herself. "He just said something crazy. It didn't make any sense to me. He said, 'Thank the Eagle for me. Thank Purcell.' What do you make of that?"

Masek turned in time to see Jennifer slump into a chair. She buried her face in her hands and sobbed. She and Masek had realized the bad news about John Lucas at the same instant. Now they both knew the good news about Jim. It was over.

Flip over for another great mystery!
THREE DAYS IN WINTER

Dear Reader:

Please let us know how you feel about Barbour Books' Christian Fiction.

1. What most influenced you to purchase Jennifer Grey Mystery Collection #1, #2, #3 (Please circle one)?

   ____ Author   ____ Recommendations

   ____ Subject matter   ____ Price

   ____ Cover / titles

2. Would you buy other books in the Jennifer Grey Mystery series by this author?

   ____ Yes   ____ No

3. Where did you purchase this book?

   ____ Christian book store   ____ Other

   ____ General book store   ____ Mail order

4. What is your overall rating of this Collection?

   ____Excellent ____ Very good ____Good ____ Fair ____ Poor

5. How many hours a week do you spend reading books? ____ hrs.

6. Are you a member of a church? ____ Yes   ____ No

   If yes, what denomination?_____

7. Please check age

   ____ Under 18   ____ 25-34   ____ 45-54

   ____ 18-24   ____ 35-44   ____ 55 and over

Mail to: **Fiction Editor**
Barbour Books
P.O. Box 1219
Westwood, NJ 07675

NAME _____

ADDRESS _____

CITY _____ STATE _____ ZIP _____

Thank you for helping us provide the best in Christian fiction!

Dear Reader:

Please let us know how you feel about Barbour Books' Christian Fiction.

1. What most influenced you to purchase Jennifer Grey Mystery Collection #1, #2, #3 (Please circle one)?

    ____ Author   ____ Recommendations

    ____ Subject matter   ____ Price

    ____ Cover / titles

2. Would you buy other books in the Jennifer Grey Mystery series by this author?

    ____ Yes   ____ No

3. Where did you purchase this book?

    ____ Christian book store   ____ Other

    ____ General book store   ____ Mail order

4. What is your overall rating of this Collection?

    ____ Excellent ____ Very good ____ Good ____ Fair ____ Poor

5. How many hours a week do you spend reading books? ____ hrs.

6. Are you a member of a church? ____ Yes ____ No

    If yes, what denomination?_____

7. Please check age

    ____ Under 18   ____ 25-34   ____ 45-54

    ____ 18-24   ____ 35-44   ____ 55 and over

Mail to: **Fiction Editor**
Barbour Books
P.O. Box 1219
Westwood, NJ 07675

NAME ————————————————————————————

ADDRESS ——————————————————————————

CITY ——————————— STATE ——— ZIP ————

Thank you for helping us provide the best in Christian fiction!

**Flip over for another great mystery!
HEARTBEAT**

Covering the police beat for the *CHICAGO DAY* leads Jennifer into a sordid crime scene. In fact, Jennifer becomes a suspect when first a child is murdered and then the suspect killer is found dead. But the clues just don't seem to fit. Piece them together yourself as you read and discover with Jennifer who Wyatt Oliver's killer really is.

THREE DAYS
IN WINTER

Jerry B. Jenkins, is the author of more than fifty books, including the popular Margo Mystery Series, co-author of the best-selling *OUT OF THE BLUE* with Orel Hershiser, and *HEDGES*. Jenkins lives with his wife Dianna, and three sons at Three-Son Acres, Zion, Illinois.

Jerry B. Jenkins

THREE DAYS
IN WINTER

Book Two In The Jennifer Grey Mystery Series

Flip over for another great
Jennifer Grey Mystery!
HEARTBEAT

BARBOUR BOOKS
Westwood, New Jersey

One

Heather Lauren. Jennifer thought it was a beautiful name, a name you might find in the social register of a North Shore debutante. Not the name of a murder victim on a police blotter in the West Side Precinct station.

"But that's where I found it," she told her boss, *Chicago Day* City Editor Leo Stanton. "The cops don't like it."

"I don't like it either," the veteran editor said, the ever-present unlit cigar jammed in his teeth. "Four years old? Where'd they find her?"

"Tied in the cellar."

"Abused?"

"Beaten, burned. Malnourished."

Leo swore. "Burned?"

Jennifer nodded, her eyes tearing.

Leo shook his head. "I've seen most everything in this business," he said. "In fact, I've seen this kinda thing before. But I never get used to it." He stood and walked around to the front of his desk, leaning back against it and crossing his arms as he stared down at Jennifer. "What're you going to do with it?"

She pressed her lips tight. "I don't know," she said, just above a whisper. "Play it straight, I guess. Quote the cops. Try to recreate how she was found. Talk to the coroner, the neighbors, check with Social Services."

Leo Stanton rolled up his sleeves and tugged at the waistband of his pullover sweater vest. He closed his eyes and let his head fall back, then reached up and slowly took off his half glasses, gently placing them on the desk beside him. "What would you do with this story if you could do whatever you wanted?" he asked.

Jennifer dropped her head and stared into her lap for several seconds. "I saw the pictures, Leo," she said.

"Hmm?"

"The photographs of Heather Lauren. Martin Grom, the Homicide Detective Sergeant on the West Side, showed them to me. I almost wish he hadn't."

"I know Grom. A good guy, right? Big man. A redhead."

"That's him."

"Gruesome photos, huh? Nothing we can use, I s'pose."

"We could use one, but not the other. She was a doll, Leo. Apparently the only good picture her mother had of her was taken at some local Park District function. The kids brought the pictures home to see if the parents wanted to buy them. Some did. Some kept them without buying them. That's what Mrs. Lauren did."

"And we can get that picture?"

"Sure."

"Get it."

"Even that picture makes me sick, Leo. It's so precious it makes me think of the horrible one I saw in Grom's office. Do I have to describe it?"

"To me? No. I don't get any more kick out of something like that than you do. In your piece, yes. The reader has to know what happened, Jennifer. You know that."

She nodded, still staring down. The old man put a hand on her shoulder. "Jennifer, you never answered my question, so I'm gonna answer it for you. I want you to whip out the straight story fast. We'll go with it on page one with the good photo. Then I want you to do a sidebar; anything you want."

"Oh, Leo, no. You won't print what I'd have to write."

"You're gonna tell me what I'd print?" he said, smiling. "Try me."

"It's not funny, Leo. It's just that I'm so angered by this thing that I don't know if I can even do the straight story without intruding on it."

"You know I can't print opinion in the straight piece, Jennifer. And I can't have you spouting off about your religion. But a little emotion, especially on a story like this, well, there's no harm in that. That's why I'm telling you to do two. Let me decide if I can print the sidebar or not. Regardless, the page one story has to be done within the hour, and you'd better send someone to the West Side to get that photograph. I don't s'pose we can scoop the *Trib* or the *Times* on the photo."

"No, but at least we won't be the only one without it, and that's saying something."

"That's saying something, all right," Stanton said, returning to his chair. "The *Trib* has Bob Greene and Dear Abby. The *Times* has Mike Royko and Gary Deeb. We're glad when we're not the only one without a hot photo. The only thing we've got is the best police reporter in town."

Jennifer would have enjoyed the compliment another day. Now she trudged to the video screen at her desk, sliding her leather shoulder bag to the floor and draping her calf-length camel hair coat over the back of the chair.

It was always hot in the newsroom. She unzipped her boots and sat in stocking feet, digging from her bag the spiral notebook containing her notes. She propped it up next to the screen, then called the West Side Precinct station house.

"Chicago Police."

"Homicide, please."

"Jis' a minute."

"Homicide, Henry."

"Sergeant Grom, please."

"He's busy. Can he call you back?"

"No, please tell him it's Jennifer Grey from the *Day*."

"Grey from the *Day* for Grom on the phone? I love it! Hang on."

"This is Grom. Hi, Jenn."

"Hi, Martin. Listen, I know you're in the middle of this thing, but can I send someone to get the picture?"

"Yeah. You wanted the Park District shot, right?"

"Of course. You're not releasing the one from the cellar, are you?"

"You want it?"

"No, but—"

"Your competitors want it."

"You're kidding!"

"Nope. The both want it."

"They going to run it?"

"You mean do they want to? I can't imagine. I'd never let it out. Would you want that photo in the paper if it was your kid?"

Jennifer thought she heard an edge in Martin Grom's voice she hadn't heard before. "You're in a mood, aren't you?" she tried.

"Ah," he said, pausing. "I got a young daughter myself. If I had it *my* way, I'd kill Wyatt Oliver right now."

Jennifer grabbed for her notebook so fast she knocked it to the floor. "You're saying you believe Cornelia Lauren's common-law husband murdered the child?"

"Oh, Jenn, you can't quote me on that, please! Can't I just spout off to you without getting my neck in a noose? I'd be assigned to the mayor's office for bug control if that came out in the paper."

"That didn't sound off-the-record to me, Martin. You know you have to tell me it's off-the-record *before* you say it, not after."

"Well, you gotta pretend I told you in time on this one, Jennifer. Don't pull any technicality on me and quote me just because I felt free to tell you what I was thinking. Promise me."

You don't have to worry, Martin. Hang on a second so I can tell Bobby ɔ go get the picture."

She signaled her assistant, Robert Block, who sat with his feet up on his desk reading *Newsweek.*

"West Side Precinct," she said. "An envelope is in my name at the desk. Get it to composition ASAP."

"Why didn't you get it when you were there?" he whined.

"They had to make copies for each of us—oh, Bobby, just hit the road, will you? Do I have to tell Leo that you're being—"

"No, but I have no doubt that you would, with half a reason."

"You waste any time getting that photo, and I'll have more than half a reason." She turned back to the phone. "Sorry, Martin. So, tell me, is Mrs. Lauren sticking with her story, or did she lead you to believe that this, uh, Oliver, uh, Wyatt Oliver guy killed Heather?"

"You're not gonna print what I said, right?"

"I promised, Martin."

"Awright. No, both she and Oliver are sticking with their story."

"And what you don't like about it is that if the daughter had really been missing for two days, they would have reported it to somebody?"

"Right."

"OK, Martin, off-the-record. If Wyatt Oliver killed the kid, why would his common-law wife cover for him?"

"Cause she's scared to death of him. Wouldn't you be?"

Jennifer thought for a moment. "I guess. I'd rather not say how I feel about him right now, because I'm afraid you're right."

"We just want to book him soon, because there's another kid in the family—you know, the seven-year-old boy."

"Elliott?"

"Right."

"Is that his real name?"

"Yeah, Elliott Lauren."

"Another beautiful name for a poor, sad child."

"Yeah, I gotta go, Jenn. I'll call you if I get anything more."

"No, you won't."

"You're right, I probly won't. But I do owe ya one. You don't print what I said about Wyatt Oliver, and I may just call you if I get anything new."

"Thanks, Martin."

Jennifer turned to her keyboard and began tapping out the front page story:

The burned, beaten, and emaciated body of a four-year-old girl was found tied to a post in the cellar of a West Side apartment building Wednesday afternoon after police responded to a call from the girl's mother, Mrs. Cornelia Lauren of 4326 W. Stivers. The Cook County coroner's office is still trying to determine the cause of death.

Mrs. Lauren, 31, who lives in the building with her common-law husband, Wyatt Oliver, 36, and her son, Elliott, 7, told police her daughter Heather had not come home from a Park District preschool program Monday afternoon. She said she discovered the body at approximately 3:30 P.M. Wednesday.

West Side Homicide Detective Sergeant Martin Grom said police had no record of a missing person's report having been filed in the case. Neighbors were apparently unaware that the girl had been missing. But Oliver, an unemployed truck driver, says he wouldn't have asked his neighbors for help anyway. Oliver and Lauren are one of few white couples in the neighborhood, and police have intervened in disputes in their building before.

When asked to explain the apparent malnourishment, Mrs. Lauren said her daughter had always been a light eater and very thin. She said that whoever had abducted the child must have inflicted the bruises and burns, because "the only time Heather ever hurt herself was when she fell down the stairs and burned herself on a hot plate."

Sergeant Grom refused to comment on any leads or suspects in the case, though he admitted that police would be questioning the couple.

Jennifer finished the article with a more detailed description of the child's injuries, along with other minor details and a menu of related articles the reader could expect over the next few days, including interviews with neighbors and acquaintances, the police, and the coroner. She transmitted the story to Leo's screen and waited.

In a few minutes her phone rang. "Remarkably detached," he said. "C'mon in."

"You can sense where my head is from the piece, though, can't you?" she asked, standing in his doorway.

" 'Course. So will the reader. But everyone will have the same suspicions. The kid is missing two days before the mother finds her? No one has been looking, let alone even knows the kid has been gone? The woman is a lousy liar, Jenn. She admits the kid fell down the stairs at age three which is unlikely—and that she got burned on a hot plate. Are we talking about a burned finger? You write here that the girl had burns and burn scars on 15 percent of her body. Maybe a kidnapper gave her the fresh burns and bruises, but burn scars? That many don't come from a hot plate unless she wrestled with the thing."

"I know. And I'm so livid I don't even want to take a shot at the sidebar."

"You don't understand, Jennifer," Leo said. "It's not a suggestion. I want that piece. If you go overboard, I'll edit you a little. Let's do it. Let's prove we know what the readers are thinking and identify with them once. People are sick and tired of people who hurt children. Let's show 'em we have the same feelings. What could you say that I wouldn't print, besides the fact that you think Jesus is the answer for everything?"

Jennifer looked pained.

"I'm sorry," Leo said. "That was a little cold."

"Not to mention a little simplistic."

"OK, guilty. But other than a sermonette, I want to see what's rattling around in your brain under all that brown hair. How 'bout it?"

Two

Jennifer padded back to her desk, still not sure what to do with the sidebar and wished she could talk to Jim before their late dinner in Geneva. But she was determined to stick with the agreement she had struck with Leo and the publisher: "You can date a police officer as long as you don't see him or talk to him when either of you are working, and provided you neither use him to gain information, nor personally handle a story in which he might be mentioned."

It was better than being reassigned to the society page, but there were days when she wondered if it was worth it. How could she not discuss this terrible story with him, just because he happened to be a policeman? She couldn't avoid it, it was as simple as that. She loved him; she needed him as a sounding board. She wouldn't be pumping him for information, and he wouldn't offer any—not even to tip her off as to who to talk to.

Her screen's red light came on. She called up the message. "Leo the Lion sez: Don't daydream too long. You've got about 40 minutes to give me the equivalent of 2 takes."

"Thanks, Mane Man," she tapped back, not feeling as light as her message. She hit the key to clear the screen and put away her notebook while the computer was doing its thing. She would do this piece off the top of her head.

She breathed a silent prayer and tried to keep her tears in check as she began:

> I saw a photograph today that made me an instant militant in the campaign for capital punishment.
>
> I don't know who beat or burned or starved or neglected four-year-old Heather Lauren to death in her own West Side basement this week, and something tells me I don't want to know.
>
> You can see the *before* picture on page one. That's her next to the grizzly headline and my just-the-facts story. If the picture were in color, you could see that she was a

blue-eyed blonde with a pageboy haircut, a shy smile, and perfect little teeth.

But the beauty of the child and the horrible manner of her death is not what moves me to temporarily leave my niche as a police reporter to tell you that I feel the same way you do about this story.

I do, but then I hope you suspected that. Maybe you didn't. Maybe you think I've grown calloused over the last two years, writing about crime, about good cops and bad cops, white-collar criminals and blue-collar criminals.

Maybe you think that to me it's all just more grist for the newspaper stories, something that allows me to fill my space, justify my existence, put food on my table. Maybe you think I can forget it and go home, only to return and hit it again the next day.

Well, I can't. I'm as depressed by bad news as you are. It affects me as much. And when I've seen the police department's photo of a lifeless little body—a photo so offensive that we wouldn't dare publish it in a family newspaper—perhaps it affects me even more than it does you.

When I leave the office after writing this article, I'll go home, I'll see my friends, I'll have dinner, I'll watch the news, I'll go to bed. And when I get up, I'll come back to work and investigate the story for days until someone is suspected, sought, found, charged, convicted, and sentenced.

And then we will all forget about Heather Lauren for awhile. Or will we? Will I? I'll see that picture again and again in my mind. I'll hear the story in court more times than I want to. And I'll be reminded constantly of the vulnerability of the child. Any child.

People who prey upon defenseless victims—the aged, the infirm, the young—should be punished. Of course, anyone who preys upon anyone else is wrong. But in the cases of the defenseless, the crimes are all the more heinous. For they are always perpetrated for the most selfish reasons.

Murderers murder the aged for their money. They murder the infirm for their money. They murder children

for their silence, or to eliminate the haunting, hungry eyes that bring guilt. Maybe they're inconvenient.

I know this isn't the right era for tough laws, for punishment at the expense of rehabilitation, for inhumane treatment of society's misfits, for not understanding the difficult environments that produce someone capable of the crime that will be on our minds for weeks.

But if you saw the picture I saw today and compared it to the one on the front page of this newspaper, you'd be unable to swallow the lump in your throat. You'd be unable to hold back the tears. You'd be frightened of your feelings. And you'd want justice.

I can't help it. I want to see the guilty party pay for this crime. And when the bleeding heart letters come pouring in to call me inhumane, I'll call to memory that photograph just one more time and know I'll never change my mind.

Jennifer transmitted the story to Leo but didn't wait for his reaction. She pulled on her boots and coat and hurried down the back corridor toward the parking lot, passing Bobby on the way. She sniffed and managed, "Get it?"

"Yes, your highness," he said. "I can handle all dese tough jobs Massa Grey, ma'am. Anything else yôu wants of Bobby today?"

She ignored him and kept moving. He had tried so hard—and almost succeeded—to get her fired for seeing Jim while handling the police beat. Bobby would graduate from Northwestern and be her boss within a few years, she guessed, unless someone was made fully aware of his attitude.

He was good at hiding it, and he did have unusual talent. But he was a scoundrel who needed exposing, and if she couldn't change him or at least get him to see that he needed changing, she'd have to pull him out from under his slimy rock to protect others.

This was one of those days when Bobby Block didn't seem worth the effort.

A light snow had covered Jennifer's little car, and she hated to think what she was doing to her coat, leaning against the salty, slushy sides of the car to scrape the windows. She wanted to look nice for Jim tonight. He would have been at prayer meeting. Someday she would have an assignment that would free her to go with him. But for now, Wednesday evenings, after she got off work, were their late dinner nights.

She always looked forward to them, no matter how tired she was. And regardless what might come up at work or how late she had to stay, Officer James Purcell would never hear of canceling. He'd wait, he always said. And he always did. Once until eleven thirty.

It wouldn't be that late tonight, but never had Jennifer been more tired or had more on her mind. She arrived at her apartment with just enough time to park, grab her mail, ride the elevator to her floor, freshen up, change clothes, and answer the doorbell. It was too early for Jim.

"You got a delivery, Miss Grey," old Mrs. Alexander yodeled. "You weren't here, and I knew you weren't here, so I told him you weren't here but that I knew you and that I would take if for you and that I would even pay him, and so I did. A dollar I gave him. For this."

Beaming, she held out a small, narrow box Jennifer dug a dollar from her purse, deciding not to open the box until Mrs. Alexander was gone. She appreciated the kindness, but the contents of the box were none of her neighbor's business.

"Thank you very much," Jennifer said, smiling. "You're so kind."

"And so is Jim," the old woman said with a twinkle as she backed down the hall. "One red rose, and so lovely!"

It was all Jennifer could do to keep from slamming the door. *The nosy old bat was right, anyway* she said to herself, sitting on the edge of the sofa opening the box. *It is lovely.*

The card read, *I'm looking forward to tonight. Pick you up at 9.*

She nearly panicked. Was there something special about this Wednesday night? Was there something she had forgotten? Was it an anniversary of sorts? She couldn't remember. Jim was thoughtful; she'd received deliveries before. But what did his card mean? Maybe nothing, but what if she'd forgotten something she should have remembered?

She put the rose in a tiny vase and scurried to finish her face and hair. *I hope he hasn't got anything up his sleeve*, she thought, surprised by how nervous and excited she always felt about seeing him again, even after a day like today.

She knew the real thing when it came along. She'd been through it before. After other experiences of puppy love and infatuation through high school and college, she'd fallen in love with Scott Grey. And it had been only recently that she had forgiven him for dying on an icy road early in their marriage.

That was why for so long she had hidden even from herself her true feelings for Jim. It couldn't be, she decided, that the first man she chose to see after finally emerging from her grief, would be a man she could love.

And so she didn't. She simply wouldn't allow herself to fall for him. Jim was patient. He knew. He understood. He waited. Bided his time. Proved himself. And when she had least expected it, her love for him burst from its hiding place.

She loved him unabashedly. And he loved her. They were unusually blessed with a relationship that lucky people approach only once in their lifetimes. He had been disappointed in love before. She had been happily married, then widowed. And now God had given them each other.

She looked at her watch. Eight fifty-five. Jim would arrive in five minutes, as usual. And she would be ready. As usual. She latched her watchband and folded her coat over her arm and sat again on the edge of the couch.

She could just as easily sleep as go out, and she realized she would not go out tonight for anyone in the world but Jim. Not even Leo. Dad? She'd probably try to beg off, but Dad could talk her into it. And if Jim was the only person besides her dad who she would go out with after an exhausting day, then that was as high a compliment as she could pay him.

She'd have done anything—and often had—for Scott too. It was good to be able to think about him rationally now. Finally. For how long had his absence been the first thing on her mind every day?

She hadn't been able to keep him from her mind, and when the memories intruded, they suffocated her with grief, longing, hoping, wishing his accident had never happened. No pleasant memory of him had ever wafted through her mind without ending in that remarkably stark and sterile conversation with the young state trooper who brought her the news that had changed her life.

Had she grown out of it, like a child who quits sucking his thumb? Had Jim taken Scott's place? No. Time, as much as she had always hated the platitude, truly had been a healer of the wound. Jim had been part of the healing process, of course, because he had not seemed threatened by her memories of Scott.

In fact, he wanted to hear about Scott. Jim felt flattered that she loved him after having been married to such an outstanding young man.

She leaped to her feet at the sound of the doorbell. There stood Jim, all tall and trim and bronze and blonde in his Ivy League earth tones, cardigan, herringbone jacket, and open trench coat.

"Hi, sweetheart," he said, smiling and reaching for her.

She embraced him. "Hi, Scott," she said, wincing immediately and knowing he was doing the same. "Jim, I'm so sorry. I've never done that before, have I?"

He chuckled. "Been thinking again?"

"Yes, but mostly about you."

"Sounds like it," he said, still smiling.

"Really I was. I love you, Jim."

"I love you too. Get anything from me today?"

"Yes, and I loved it. It worried me though."

"Worried you?"

"Yes, have I forgotten something? Is there something special about this day or this dinner? If there is, I'm sorry, but it's passed me by."

"Does it have to be a special occasion for me to remind you that I look forward to dinner with you?" he said, reaching behind her and pulling the door shut, then walking her to the elevator.

"No, it's great, but if I forgot something, you remind me."

"What would you forget?"

"The first time we held hands or kissed or something."

"You mean we've already held hands and kissed?" he said, mocking, as the elevator door shut.

She planted a passionate one on him. "Now we have," she said, laughing.

He wrapped his arm tightly around her as they stepped into a frigid wind. "You look tired," he said.

"More than usual on Wednesday night?"

"Yeah. 'Fraid so. Tough day?"

"Always."

"But more so than usual?"

"How'd you know?"

"I know everything."

"You know about the little girl on the West Side, of course."

"Of course."

"You mind if we don't talk about it?"

"Whatever you want, Jenn." He opened the car door for her. "I would have thought you might want to bounce it off me, though," he said, shutting it.

"I thought so too," she said when he slid behind the wheel. "In fact, I've been looking forward to talking to you about it all afternoon. Now I want to talk about anything but."

He gave her an understanding glance and pulled away into the night toward the western suburbs.

Three

Jim insisted on taking Jennifer home early when she nearly dozed off at dinner. He hadn't pressed her about her reactions to the Heather Lauren murder, but she did reveal why she felt she couldn't talk about it.

"I emptied myself in a sidebar, a personal column type thing, Jim. I think the Lord really gave me clarity of mind, because it came out just the way I wanted it to. I really don't know if I could have expressed it better, and I sure won't try to do it from memory. You'll see it in the morning *Day.* Let me know what you think."

"I can hardly wait. I know what I'll think. I'll think it's great, like all your stuff."

"You don't understand, Jim. This is so forthright that it may get me into trouble with the readership. In fact, for all I know, Leo might not even print it. I all but demand capital punishment for the perpetrator."

"You won't get any argument from my side of the street."

"Yeah, but everybody knows you cops are right-wing red-necks. We journalists are supposed to be liberal left-wingers, remember?"

Jennifer didn't protest the early end to the evening. It was the type of attention she appreciated so much in Jim. After praying and reading some Scripture, she mentally plotted her afternoon tasks for the next day. She'd start with the Park District preschool teacher, then contact the social worker assigned to the family. If that didn't give her enough for the next morning's paper, a last minute check with Sergeant Grom would.

But the next day came earlier than Jennifer expected. Leo called shortly after 9:00 A.M. "No, it's all right, Leo, I was just getting up—in an hour or two."

"Sorry, but the big boss wants to see us in about an hour. Can you make it?"

"I dunno. How important is this guy to my career? Tell 'im I'm still in bed."

"You're cute."

"See you in forty-five, Leo. What's he want, anyway? You know?"

"Yeah, but I can't tell ya."

17

"Wonderful. Should I think raise or welfare?"

"Think anything you want; just get over here."

"You print the sidebar, Leo?"

"Didn't change a word."

"That mean you like it?"

"What do you think, Einstein?"

"Your kind of compliment. Thanks."

Max Cooper's office was on the top floor of the *Day* building on Michigan Avenue. Even Leo appeared nervous.

"This is Jennifer Grey," Leo said.

"Of course, sure," the tall, thin, intense, distinguished publisher said. He had a reputation for looking good but being a little rough around the edges in personality. "I shook hands with you at the Christmas party, didn't I?"

"No, I wasn't there. But I've seen you around, of course."

"Of course, and I know your stuff. Sit down, sit down."

Cooper joined Leo and Jennifer at a small wood table and grinned at them. *If my career has just bit the dust, he's pretty happy about it,* Jennifer decided.

"Let me get straight to the point, Miss Grey. I was serious about knowing your stuff. I read you every day, and I mean that. If you don't believe it, just quiz me."

"I believe you."

"Good, 'cause who knows how I'd do on a fool quiz! Ha!"

Leo laughed. Jennifer smiled. Cooper continued.

"I, ah, was a police reporter myself when I started out. 'Course, my old man owned the whole chain, so I sorta had my pick, if you know what I mean." Jennifer nodded. "But anyway, I've always kept a close eye on the police beat."

"Don't I know it?" Leo said.

"Yeah! You hear from me about that now and then, don't you, Lion? I call him Lion all the time, don't I, Lion?" Leo nodded. "Well, Leo here was a police reporter way back when too. Seems all the really good guys start there."

Jennifer smiled at Max Cooper, enjoying whatever it was he was trying to say.

"Now me, before I went administrative, I went from the police beat to the sports page, then sports columnist and sports editor. I don't s'pose you've got any aspirations that way, do you, Miss Grey?"

"No, not really."

"Well, 'course not. Not that a woman couldn't do a good job in sports. Wouldn't be against that at all if a qualified one wanted to or whatever, right? But you don't want that."

"No, sir."

"Well, I said I was going to get straight to the point, didn't I? I've been following your stuff for some time, and I've seen a spark there. I've seen attention to detail. I've seen a sensitivity there. I've seen the color, the depth, the care—the types of things that most people wouldn't think an old hack like me would notice if they stared him in the face."

"Thank you, sir."

"Well, thank you. I mean, let's put the credit where the credit's due. Anyway, I've been pushing on the Lion here to get you into a little more feature stuff, not tryin' to tell him his job or anything, but just to see what your potential is. 'Course Leo agrees with me anyway; fact is, he saw you were special long before I did and told me so. You've got an ally there, Miss Grey."

Jennifer smiled at Leo and refrained from telling Cooper that she was actually a *Mrs.*, as she usually did.

"Well, anyway, I didn't know what Leo had done this morning when I saw your sidebar on the little girl's murder. I mean, I wanted him to broaden your horizons a little, and you may have sensed he's been doing that, but letting you go and get so personal and opinionated and, uh, uh, earthy there—why, I just didn't know what to expect."

"How did you feel about it, Mr. Cooper?" Jennifer asked.

"Me? Well, there wasn't anything wrong with your position as far as I'm concerned. I mean, I s'pose it's the type of thing I would have had no problem with on the editorial page or in some signed column or something. You were speaking my mind there, Miss Grey, and everybody's I assume, except for some misguided do-gooders who think more of the criminal than of the victim."

"So, you don't feel it should have been placed next to the end of the story on page three?"

"I'm not saying that. I'm saying that I didn't know what to think when I saw it. I was moved by it, I must tell you that. I cried reading it, and I don't cry reading anything! The last time a newspaper piece moved me to tears was when Bob Greene did that thing in the *Trib* last year directed to the Tylenol killer. But I also must tell you that as soon as I got myself under control again, I was wearing my publisher's hat, and I started to worry. And I wanted to know why Leo had had you do it. I wasn't going to blame you. I was going to have the Lion's hide here if the phones started ringin' off the wall from the ACLU or who knows who else."

Jennifer was puzzled. What exactly was the man trying to say?

"I know what you're thinking, Miss Grey. I know you're thinking that it's awful small of me to decide who gets called on the carpet and who doesn't, based on what the readers think of what goes in the paper. And you're right. But it's the name of the game. If they like it, I'm happy. If enough of 'em don't like it, then we've got trouble, whether I agree with the article or not. Which, as I already told you, I do.

"You see, we're still the third paper in a town with three papers, and I gotta tell ya, we're not ignoring the *Defender*, which a lot of people don't think qualifies as one of the biggies. It's comin' on, and we may be a town with four major papers again one day.

"But we thought Chicago could use another daily, even when the *Today* and the *Daily News* couldn't compete. Everybody knows we've succeeded, and we've hurt the competition—at least we've taken some of their readers and advertisers. Personally, I think competition can only help a paper, unless it runs it out of business. And we have no intention of doing that.

"So, as tough and honest and real as I want our paper to be, we still have to be a little conservative in our policies so we don't lose big batches of readers at a time. One or two over a mistake or disagreement once in a while, OK. But not hundreds of readers at a crack. Can't afford it."

"And is that what's happening this morning, Mr. Cooper?"

The big boss squinted at her and then at Leo Stanton. He rose and smiled. "No, ma'am. Apparently you haven't been listening to the radio, watching the news, noticing the newspaper stands. Our pressrun ran out, Miss Grey. It *ran out*! Do you know the last time a daily paper in this town had to go back to press with the same edition, Miss Grey? Neither do I. You struck a nerve, lady. You hit big. You're the talk of the town. People want today's issue of the *Day*. And you know what that means? That means they're going to want tomorrow's, and the next day's, and the next—long as there's a personal column by you in there."

Suddenly the man fell silent and sat again. Jennifer took it as her cue to rise. Both Cooper and Stanton were content to let her be the next to speak. They looked at each other and smiled. But she was troubled.

"Can I ask a question?" she said.

"Absolutely," Cooper said.

"What would I be hearing right now if the reaction had been the opposite?"

"Good question, young lady. And I want to be honest with you. You see, you and I think a lot alike; I could tell that from your previous work, but especially in your column this morning. I like you; I like what you say. But if the public reaction had been negative, you wouldn't be standing here

right now. Stanton would have been in trouble, and you would have been put out to pasture somewhere until this thing blew over."

"If you don't mind my saying so, that sounds like a pretty shaky way to start a relationship as a columnist. Right or wrong, the public decides, correct?"

"It's a business, Miss Grey."

"Mrs. Grey."

"Excuse me."

"That's all right. So if I become a daily columnist and the public suddenly decides it doesn't like me, I'm through?"

"I know how that sounds, Miss, ah, Mrs. Grey."

"But that's the case."

"Yes, that's the case."

"I'll have to think about it."

"Columnists don't get Guild rates, Mrs. Grey. We pay them like executives. For you, that would mean nearly a 50 percent increase in pay."

"Because of one emotional column?"

"Of course not. I told you, I've been reading you."

"But the public reaction tipped the scales."

"That's right," Cooper said, suddenly sobering. "Listen, sit down and let me tell you something, Mrs. Grey. If Leo hadn't told me a little about you, you can understand how I could be a little offended by your reaction here."

"Yes, sir, I know, but it's just that—"

"I know. I know you're not motivated by money or power or prestige."

"I'm not above being flattered by all that, but—"

"I know you're a religious person and that—"

"I prefer not to refer to my faith as religion."

"Whatever, I know you're a churchgoing person and honest and all that."

"And that would have to come through in any column I would write. Not in every column, but if you want my personality on paper, that would have to be a factor."

Cooper furrowed his brow. "It wasn't overt in the column this morning."

"No, but I did pray about writing that."

"Well, listen. If the public goes for it, you can write sermons for all I care. I'm not a man without principles myself, but I need a columnist the people want to read, and right now they want to read you, so you're it. It's yours if you want it. I'll have Leo put you on the bottom of page one, just like Keegan in the *Trib*. You can write what you want, but I assume you'd stay on this Heather Lauren case until it's resolved."

"You may find that that's what got everyone so excited today. Not me, but the case itself."

"Well, you may be right. I don't think so, but who knows? If you're right, the public will let us know, and you'll be back on the police beat."

"Just like that?"

"Just like that. And let me ask you something. Where do you think Greene or Deeb or even Royko would be if the public suddenly decided they weren't worth the price of the paper every day?"

Jennifer blinked. "But they don't write what the public wants to hear just to keep their jobs."

"And we wouldn't want you to do that either. Just be yourself. As long as they love you, we'll have a tough time keeping you from jumping to one of the other papers."

"Can I think about it?"

"For how long?"

"Twenty-four hours?"

"On one condition. You do at least one more piece like today's for tomorrow morning's paper."

"I'm not sure I've got anything more to say like that."

"It doesn't have to be just like it. Do your usual digging on the story today, write a straight piece, and then do a reflective sidebar. Where is your head since you wrote the last one and turned up more evidence? That type of thing is what the readers want to know."

"I'll try," Jennifer said.

Leo clapped. "That's what she said last night, Max. Just before she wrote the winner."

Four

Jennifer's mind was jumbled as she swung off Bilford Boulevard onto the long and depressing Stivers Avenue. Just to drink in the atmosphere, she started four blocks from Lake Michigan and drove through more than eight miles of stoplights, crowded intersections, and elevated train underpasses from West Stivers.

She would have to have a talk with Leo. She had to smile at old man Cooper calling him Lion. Not Leo the Lion. Not The Lion. Just Lion. For how long had Leo been setting her up for this column possibility?

Already she'd heard on the radio that she wasn't exactly the hit of the *entire* town as Max Cooper had hoped. Indeed, the ACLU had released a statement demanding a retraction or an apology or a modification from her.

And there were rumors that another columnist, on her own paper, would be taking issue with her in the next edition. She wondered how Cooper would react to that. And what if Cooper was right, that *she* had hit the nerve, and thus her counterpart would be taking an unpopular stand? Would that mean a soon end of his stint as a columnist?

The ACLU thing had initiated a mini-barrage of callers telling a radio talk show host that they agreed she'd been wrong. If she hadn't been bolstered by the reactions of so many others, including her boss and his boss, she might have panicked, wondered if she had done the right thing, looked for a way out.

But she didn't even have to ask to see again the photo Martin Grom had showed her in the West Side Precinct station house the day before. She could remember. Would she ever be able to forget?

Jennifer had a 1:00 P.M. appointment with Angela Liachi, Heather Lauren's preschool supervisor. But with a little time to spare, she made a quick decision. She was going to drop in on Heather's mother and, she hoped, Wyatt Oliver.

She was ten minutes finding a parking place on the street, and then she wasn't confident her locked car was any more secure than if she had left the keys in it.

As she headed toward 4326, she heard the whistles and catcalls of groups of men she'd seen huddled around burning trash cans, bouncing on their toes, hands jammed in their pockets except when lighting cigarettes.

Such groups dotted all of Stivers Avenue from just west of the Loop all the way through the high-rise projects and into the low-rise duplexes. Now she was into the rows of three-story, full-basement apartments that teemed with occupants, usually more than one family per apartment, at least two apartments per floor.

Jennifer fingered a can of chemical spray in her right coat pocket. Her purse strap was wrapped around her left arm. In her left hand she clutched her key ring, which contained a police whistle and a tiny razor blade that could be exposed with one snap of the wrist.

She could blind one, slice one, and scare a few with the whistle, but she didn't want to have to. She never had before, and now she simply wished she'd dressed less bourgeois. What was it Jim had advised, besides all the artillery? "Walk as if you know where you're going, as if you're expected any second, and as if you just might be a cop."

More important, she thought, *as to actually know and to actually be expected, and to actually be a cop.* Except for knowing where she was going, she had two strikes. If she didn't get an answer at the Oliver-Lauren residence, it was a good walk back to the car with at least one group of bored, unemployed men between it and her.

When she stole a glance back at them, however, it was apparent they had already given up on her. Now she noticed groups of preschool age children—some school age—frolicking near chain link fences in a world of gray and brown.

Jennifer looked at her watch. Almost twelve-thirty. Not much time. But then she probably wouldn't need much.

She sensed the eyes of many neighbors as she approached the front door of the dingy three-floor apartment building. The sign at the front read, "Use Side Entrance." She didn't like the looks of the dark space between buildings that led to the side door.

What was left of a crumbling sidewalk echoed under her boots as she moved around the building. The wind picked up momentum in the small passageway, hidden from the sun. She gritted her teeth at the bone-chilling gusts and wondered about the makeshift screens on the windows and doors.

There were no storm windows, nor—she assumed—any insulation. The screen door at the side was loose on its hinges, and giant tears top and bottom made it worthless for the summer, let alone the winter.

Jennifer sensed no movement from inside the building, though she knew someone had to be home in at least one of the apartments. She was about to revert back to Plan A and drive the few blocks to locate Angela Liachi when she was startled by the rattlecrashing bursting open of the side door.

A tiny, sandy-haired boy, the size of a four- or five-year-old ran past her. "Are you Elliott?" she called after him.

He nodded once as he ran, not looking back. He accelerated and turned a corner out of her sight. "Is your mother home?" she called again, but suddenly the entire neighborhood was silent. Even the wind seemed to have stopped. It was as if no one could believe she had come there in her hotshot ensemble with her camel coat and her leather boots and her cover-girl makeup and her shining hair and then had the audacity to ask for someone.

Her eyes darted out from the darkness into the harsh sunlight that lit but didn't warm the street. The men were turning back to their oil drum fire. The kids stared at her from across the street. She waited until they lost interest and turned back to their games. Then she knocked on the warped wood of the screen door.

She felt conspicuous. Watched. Unwanted.

She pulled at the squeaky door and reached in to knock more loudly on the inner door, which wasn't in much better shape. The first firm tap of her knuckles pushed the door all the way open. Stunned, she stepped back and waited. Nothing.

Looking around one more time, Jennifer stepped inside and carefully shut the door behind her, feeling foolish. To her left, the stairs led to the cellar. To the right was an open archway into the kitchen of one of the first floor flats. Straight ahead, the stairs led up. Heather Lauren's family lived on the second floor.

It seemed to her to take ages to make up her mind. She decided that Sergeant Martin Grom would soon convince a judge that he had enough on Wyatt Oliver and Cornelia Lauren to hold them and maybe even charge them with child abuse, manslaughter, murder, or whatever he wanted. She would then be unable to interview them.

She poked her head into the kitchen on the first floor. "Anyone home?" she called quietly.

No response, even though she smelled food cooking.

She headed upstairs, holding her breath, listening for any sound of life. She knocked at a door, but footsteps on the third floor, resounding through the ceiling, scared her off. She hurried back down to the first floor and waited by the side door again.

There was no sound of steps on the stairs, so she crept down to the cellar. The musty dampness, combined with the stench of a makeshift

bathroom where drunks apparently detoured before staggering into their apartments at night, nauseated her.

She located an area surrounding a simple metal pole that had been roped off by the police. There was no sign of a struggle or of blood, but a blunted chalk tracing around the base of the pole marked where Cornelia Lauren told police she had found the tied, slumped body of her daughter.

Jennifer felt the bile rise in her throat and the anger shorten her breath. Why wouldn't someone have heard the girl's cries? Where were the first-floor families when this happened? Where were they now?

She pressed her lips tight and hunched her shoulders against the chill, walking as close to the police rope as she could and peering into the shadows to try to imagine the scene. The memory of the horrible photo flooded her mind and she realized for the first time that it had been taken before the little body had been cut free.

Dear God, she prayed silently, fighting tears, *here's one I'll never understand. If it had to happen for some reason, at least help us find who did it.*

The sound of footsteps on the stairs above her froze Jennifer to her spot. Through the back of the stairs she could see bare feet and what appeared to be old, charcoal-colored suit pants. There was no exit except those stairs and nowhere to hide either.

Was he coming down to see if someone was there? Or because he knew someone was there? Or for a reason totally unrelated? The time for ducking behind something was past. She stood her ground and squinted at the small, muscley figure that had stopped at the bottom of the steps.

He glared at her without a word. He was not armed. His fingers were entwined in those Salvation Army barrel suit pants, holding them up for want of a belt. He wore a ribbed, sleeveless undershirt.

The light from the basement window shone on the back of his head, leaving his face dark, so Jennifer moved to her right to get a better look. His hair was long, greasy, and unkempt. He was unshaven. His eyes looked back. His muscles were taut.

Jennifer imagined she could smell him from ten feet away. She decided not to speak first. He spread his feet apart, as if ready to defend his position.

He looked Italian; he spoke with what Jennifer guessed was a trained phony Southern accent, like a truck driver using a CB. "The las' female found in this cellar was dead," he said.

"I don't intend to be found here," she said, surprising herself.

"Don't be too sure."

She switched to the offensive, trying to sound friendlier. "I, uh, was looking for the Lauren farmily. Mr. Oliver. Mrs. Lauren. Their son."

"Dawn here you was lookin' for 'em?"

"Upstairs too. I didn't see anyone."

"You knock?"

"Yes, sir."

"I don't answer the door, an' my wife is in mournin'."

"Are you also?"

"Ma'am?"

"Are you also in mourning, Mr. Oliver?"

"You want trouble, lady?" He swore. "Who are you anyway?"

"Jennifer Grey. I write for the *Chicago Day* newspaper. Are you familiar with it?"

"I can't afford no newspaper. We ain't even paid off the TV yet."

"Did you beat your wife's daughter, Mr. Oliver?"

His eyes narrowed. "I think you better get your little self outta my house."

"Is this your building?"

"I live here."

"You own this basement?"

"Don't make me throw you out, writer lady."

"Unless you have a weapon, you'll not be throwing me anywhere," Jennifer said, her heart smashing against her ribs. "Or are you going to tie me to a post and burn me and punch me?"

His hand shook. "Are *you* armed, lady?"

"Yes, sir."

He eyed her warily, then spoke softly. "I'm bettin' you're lyin'," and he moved quickly toward her.

Jennifer yanked both hands from her pockets simultaneously, flicking open the razor blade in her left hand, chemical spray poised in her right. Wyatt Oliver instinctively raised his hands in surrender, but he grabbed at his waistband again as his pants started to fall. And Jennifer dashed past him, up the stairs, out the door, down the block, and, trembling as she fumbled with her keys, slid into her car. She didn't dare even look back as she sped toward the Park District center.

She pulled into the parking area a few minutes ahead of schedule and dropped her head to the steering wheel, closing her eyes and trying to calm herself. *If that was my answered prayer, Lord,* she prayed wryly, *it could have waited.*

As she caught her breath, someone knocked on the window. Without thinking or looking up, she jammed the key back into the ignition and turned it on, throwing the car into reverse.

But as she whirled around to guide the car out of the lot, she saw a short, dark-haired woman leap clear of the car, arms outstretched, terrified. Jennifer hit the brake and rolled down her window with an embarrassed smile. "Angela?"

"Miss Grey?" Angela said. "What's got you spooked?"

"Not what. Who."

"OK. Who?"

"Wyatt Oliver."

"Why doesn't that surprise me?" Angela asked.

"Doesn't it?" Jennifer said. "Tell me about it."

"On one condition. You've got to get out from behind the wheel."

Five

Angela Liachi was cute in a plump sort of way. Short. Dark. Intense. Fast-talking. New Yorkish. Her eyes shown as she smiled at Jennifer's jumpiness.

"Thought I was Wyatt Oliver, didja?"

Jennifer nodded.

"Let's take a walk. I don't wanna be anywhere near yer car, if you know what I mean."

They walked three blocks north to the parking lot of a boarded up former fast-food restaurant where they slowed and moseyed around the building, turning their collars up against the wind. They ignored occasional honks and waves of passersby who thought they might be hookers.

"I saw your article today," Angela said, stopping and facing the sun, squinting and enjoying the little heat she could drink from it.

Jennifer put a foot up on a cracked concrete carstop and studied the ground. "Yeah? Kinda extreme, huh?"

"Are you kidding? If there was anything wrong with it, it was only that it was probly too easy."

Jennifer shot her a double take. "Too easy? You ever try writing?"

"Nah, I don't mean the writing part of it. I mean taking the position. Too easy. Who could disagree?"

"The ACLU."

Angela smiled a rueful smile and made an obscene gesture. "Bleeding heart liberals."

"People say social workers like you are bleeding heart liberal idealists," Jennifer said.

"Oh, they do, huh? Well, I don't consider myself a social worker, a bleeding heart, or a liberal."

"An idealist."

"Dyed in the wool."

The women smiled at each other.

"I have many questions for you about Heather Lauren—"

"And Wyatt Oliver, right?"

"Of course, if you know anything—"

"If I *know* anything! I could write you an article on Wyatt Oliver."

"I was going to say that I had a lot of questions for you about the case, and I appreciate your agreeing to see me, but first I wanted to talk about you."

That made Angela nervous. She started moving again, and Jennifer had to shift her weight quickly and get going to keep up. Angela swore. "It's cold," she added.

"It's nothing personal," Jennifer said. "I'm just curious."

"And you're not gonna print anything in the paper about me, are you?"

"No. Well, I might quote you on the Heather Lauren case, that's all."

"You can't quote everything I say about that. You wouldn't want to."

"We'll get to it. First, just tell me—"

"I know what you're going to ask."

"How do you know what I'm going to ask?" Jennifer was smiling, but becoming exasperated.

"Because I get it all the time. I gotta tell ya, I'm not good copy. Every few months, some well-dressed—nothing personal—reporter from some magazine or newspaper or radio or TV station comes into my little ghetto here and asks me what motivates me. That's the big word. *Motivation.* Tell me the truth, is that what you were going to ask?"

"Yes."

"Still want an answer?"

"I must have missed all those interviews you've done. I've never heard or read your answer."

"That's because they never use it. I don't give 'em enough."

"And if you did, you wouldn't let them print it or broadcast it, am I right?"

"That's not it, Miss, uh, Grey—"

"Call me Jennifer, please."

"Okay, Jennifer please," she said, smiling. "The point is that I don't have any grand story to tell. Why would a skilled, privileged, educated, established, unlimited-future type like me come to the seediest part of Chicago and—they always put this in quotes—*give her life* to the blacks, Hispanics, and poor whites?"

"It's a good question, Angela. If all those reporters from all those different media ask it, it must be because they believe the public wants to know."

"But Jennifer, it would be a good question only if there was a good answer. I'd love to be able to spin a yarn for you, tell you that despite my privileged upbringing, a chance encounter with a not-so-fortunate person

taught me the meaning of selfless love. I can't. Didn't happen. I'm not a socialist. I'm not religious; I wasn't called here. I just heard about the opportunity, thought it fit me, and it seemed like the right thing to do at the time."

"How long have you been here?"

"Eight years."

"Eight years! That's got to be some kind of a record, doesn't it?"

"For one program in one neighborhood, it is. By almost double."

"You're proud of that, I can tell."

"Granted."

"Why?"

"I don't know. I came here to do a job, and I'm doin' it. Does there have to be more than that? You see how unpublishable that is?"

"I'd publish it."

"And break your promise?"

"No, I mean I would if you'd let me."

"I won't."

"I figured that. Does anything make you angry?"

"I'm pretty even, Jennifer. I've seen it all here. I've been disappointed at slow progress. I miss kids when I feel I've gotten somewhere with them and then the parents move them away in the middle of the night to stay a step ahead of their creditors."

"Is this job dangerous?"

"Yeah, but I don't want to talk about that either. I live in the neighborhood. I'm known. I use lots of locks on the door. I don't own a car. I don't go out alone at night. If I was jumped or my place invaded, I'd give whoever it was anything they wanted. I survive. I've got friends."

"Do you arm yourself?"

"No, but I'll bet *you* do."

"I do," Jennifer admitted.

"Right again."

"Are you bitter, cynical?"

"Some. Hard not to be here. Aren't you, after spending a little time here?"

"Yes. You know, Angela, I asked you what I wanted to ask you, but I feel like I haven't found out anything. You're not the typical visionary, but something must make you tick, keep you here, motivate you—sorry."

"It's all right. I knew you'd get back to it. I love the kids. I don't know why. I honestly don't know why I love the kids. There was nothing in my background that pointed me this way. I was an only child. I studied literature at Alfred University. I had no degree in this kind of work, no

training. I just applied. Not much competition, I can tell you that. We done with me?"

"I guess, but you fascinate me."

"That embarrasses me."

"I wouldn't have guessed that anything embarrasses you."

"I cover well. You've already gotten more out of me than anyone else ever did, and you promised not to use it. So let's quit wasting your time and talk about Heather Lauren."

"I don't consider it a waste of my time, but I don't want to waste yours."

"Talking about me wastes my time, but I'm not angry. I'm flattered. But I've also done enough of it."

It hadn't been said unkindly, but Jennifer got the message. "Why did you agree to talk with me about Heather?"

"Because Wyatt Oliver murdered her, and I'd like to see him fry for it."

"You *know* he did it?"

"I'd lay odds."

"Why?"

"The man is no good. I'm supposed to be used to his kind of people, but not everybody who has the misfortune to live around here is Wyatt Oliver's kind of person. His wife, for instance. She's limited."

"Limited?" Jennifer asked, taking Angela by the arm and leading her around a corner of the boarded up building to get out of the direct wind.

"Psychologically. She makes me mad, but I can sympathize with her."

"I'm sorry, I'm not following you."

"The woman is scared to death of Oliver. She needs him, she thinks, but she brings in more money than he does, which isn't much. He terrorizes her and the children, and she won't lift a finger. The cops have been over a time or two. But when the woman won't press charges, they lose interest in responding to the neighbors' calls when they've finally had enough of the screaming. You wonder where the other tenants were when that precious child was murdered in the basement?"

Jennifer nodded, but Angela's voice had broken and her chin quivered, and she couldn't speak. Jennifer tried to give her time to recover. "Yes, that's exactly what I thought when I was in the basement and saw where it had happened. It's an old rickety building, and the sound would carry. No one heard anything?"

"Have you asked them?" Angela managed. "That's part of your job, isn't it?"

"I will be asking, if I dare go back there."

Angela crossed her arms and raised her chin, closing her eyes, then opening them and lowering her gaze to Jennifer's. "I want to tell you that

I'm used to the kinds of things that go on around here. I know the frustration, the sense of emptiness, the futility. I know why women stay with men they shouldn't and why teenagers do dope and pull robberies and why men come home drunk every night and can't keep jobs. I know why families scream at each other and fight and throw things."

She was becoming emotional again, but this time Jennifer just let her regain her composure in her own time. Angela turned sideways to Jennifer and leaned a shoulder against the building.

"I understand why the cops have to cruise the area and why they have to keep people from killing each other. But there's something I don't understand. I don't understand a woman, the real parent to her children, letting anyone lay a hand on them. Isolated instances, okay. Fits of rage, forgivable once in a great while. And I know a drunken bum, many times stronger than a woman, can intimidate her to the point where she feels powerless to help herself. But if he beat the kids one night, wouldn't you be hitting the bricks the next day, first chance you got?"

Jennifer nodded; she was moved. Angela fell silent, and Jennifer didn't know where to go from there. She had a feeling Angela wasn't finished, and she knew she'd have to ask again if Angela had any hard evidence against Wyatt Oliver.

In an uncharacteristic loss of concentration, Jennifer suddenly found herself wishing she didn't have to wait until Friday night to see Jim. She missed him. She wanted to talk with him about the column possibility. But they had limited themselves to Wednesdays and weekends.

She scolded herself for even thinking about that now. Angela was staring into the distance. Interesting woman, Jennifer decided. *She gets emotional but she doesn't lose control. She doesn't break down.*

"Elliott came to the preschool program first," Angela said suddenly. "They had moved in from the South somewhere, and he was supposed to be in kindergarten. I didn't ask any questions. He was a good kid, quiet, but often short of energy and hungry.

"We give the kids milk, and once a week we get day-old pastries from one of the local bakeries. All the kids love 'em, of course, but Elliott inhaled 'em. I mean, he'd eat five or six. Every time I turned around, he'd sneak another. At first I was afraid he'd get sick, but then I feared it was all he was getting to eat."

"Not a very good diet," Jennifer said.

"Better than nothing. So I started smuggling him fruit. Terribly small, thin child, but when he got some food in him, he loved to run."

"He ran past me this morning."

"Yeah? The old man is feeding him good since Heather's been gone. Keeping him quiet is my guess."

"What makes you so sure about Oliver?"

"I've visited that place more than once. It's a hole, but I'm used to that. What I didn't like was that Wyatt Oliver didn't care that I was there; he treated his woman and her children the same as always. They waited on him hand and foot. They brought him beer and snacks, and he sat in front of a little color TV that must have cost him a month's unemployment money."

"He says he's still paying for it."

"I'll bet he is. Probably stole it. Anyway, I suggested that Heather was old enough to come to the program and also that it would be a good idea to be sure they had a good lunch on preschool days because we had so much activity. Mrs. Lauren appeared to understand, but Oliver was incensed. "You just make 'em behave there, and we'll make 'em behave here."

"I didn't know what that had to do with a good lunch, so I told him I'd never had a bit of trouble with Elliott and that I assumed I wouldn't with Heather either. He told me to just let him know if I did and I'd never have any more trouble."

"Scary."

"I should say. Scared me. I wanted to adopt both kids right then and there. Both so cute. Heather started coming to the Monday-Wednesday-Friday group after that. I couldn't get her to say a word to anyone, not even 'Hi.' But she always came. Would sometimes laugh at the stories, always participated in games. But my first clue of what was happening in that home was when we had an outing at the Y."

"A swimming party?"

"Right. A lot of the kids didn't even have suits, so they were provided by the Y. It was a bring-your-lunch-and-spend-the-day type of a thing. The Lauren kids didn't bring suits and wouldn't accept suits, either. That was the first time I heard Heather talk.

"I sat them down and told them how much fun they'd be missing, and I asked Elliott to tell me why they didn't want to swim. He looked past me as if he hadn't heard. I asked him again. He ignored me.

"I asked him again, and Heather piped up. 'We got ouchies,' she said, and Elliott leaped to his feet and screamed at her, 'Don't tell! Don't tell! Don't tell! Don't tell!'"

Six

By the time Jennifer left Angela Liachi a couple of hours later, she had heard the full story of Angela's encounters with Wyatt Oliver.

After that day at the Y, when Angela had been forced to let Elliott and Heather just sit and watch the others, because—she assumed—they had sores on their bodies where people couldn't see them, she called the Department of Social Services.

"I talked to the woman there I deal with a lot. Nathalie Benedict. She set up a bogus physical exam for my group one Friday, sort of swooped in, pulled each kid behind a screen, and had a doctor check their pulses, look down their throats, and put a stethoscope to their bare chests.

"The idea was that the doctor would be so quick and intimidating that he could just whip through the exam and at the end tug their shirts up for a quick listen. By then, Elliott wasn't coming anymore. He'd started kindergarten.

"Little Heather, who hadn't spoken to me before or after the incident at the Y, kept looking at me fearfully as she stood in line, waiting for her turn with the doctor. Her huge, sad eyes begged me to rescue her, but I alternately ignored her or smiled at her to boost her courage.

"The woman from Social Services knew which one they were really after, and she played it just right. She just ushered Heather in and spoke softly and encouragingly to her, and when the time came to lift her little shirt, Heather flinched, but let the doctor do it.

"Heather came out teary and scowled at me, as if I should have protected her from that indecency, but I didn't know if they'd found anything or what."

"Did she make you feel guilty?"

"Hardly. The whole scheme was for her benefit. She couldn't know that, but I did it for her, and I wasn't about to feel bad about it. I was sorry she had to be embarrassed, but better embarrassed than killed in her own home."

"Did they find anything?"

Angela had started walking back toward the center. "I knew when it was all over and they were putting their equipment away. The kids, for the most part, had loved it. No shots. Quick and painless. They'd been tickled. They asked questions. The doctor stayed and answered a few, but it was obvious to me that both the doctor and Nathalie were upset; it showed all over their faces. They were grim. Boiling. They waited in the parking lot until the class was over and the kids started home."

"What had they found?"

Angela stopped and faced Jennifer. "Sores. Burns. Burn scars." She bit her lip and looked down. "I was angry, so mad I was going to run after Heather and keep her from going home. Nathalie had to calm me down. She said I could cause more trouble by doing that right then. She said there was no way to immediately pull a child from her home and that if we tried, the parents would get her back and punish her worse for telling on them.

"I didn't care. I wanted to grab the kid and hide her somewhere. You had to have seen this girl, Jennifer, to know what I mean. So quiet, so sweet, so giving and loving and lovable. Short cropped blonde hair, skinny little arms and legs. Never wore dresses or skirts. Always jeans. Probably owned one pair."

Jennifer put her hand on Angela's shoulder. "You through talking for today?"

Angela shook her head. "I want to finish this. I pushed Social Services to file a report and press charges, and I know they did, but it took so long that I took matters into my own hands."

"Meaning?"

"I visited Heather's home again. When Elliott saw me, he headed for the hills."

"Elliott?"

"Yup. He knew that whatever had started that day at the Y was coming to a head, and he didn't want to get punished for letting the cat out of the bag."

"What did you do, Angela—just confront Oliver?"

"No, I wasn't dumb enough to do that. Might as well have though; I didn't fool him. I said I wanted to talk about Heather's progress. He ignored me and just sat there watching his TV. Cornelia sat with me, looking fearful, as if she wanted me to finish and get going.

"I talked about general things, motor skills, Heather's shyness, that type of stuff. Then I said that it was apparent she'd been hurt somehow and that it hampered her during playtime. I just threw it out there without comment, hoping that her mother would at least try to explain it, even with a lie."

"She didn't?"

"She shot a terrified glance at Oliver and fell silent. I mean silent. She hardly moved. I said, 'Well, is she recovering from whatever happened, or would you like me to arrange for treatment? It'll be free.' With that, Oliver wrenched around in his chair and swore at me.

"He said, 'We can take care of our own here, and we don't need any charity. Just let the kid be. She's all right. Just quit babying her.' "

"He was admitting she'd been hurt," Jennifer said.

"I thought so, and it made me mad. Maybe he could see through my offer and caught the veiled threat that if something didn't stop in that household, I was going to city authorities. I knew I was about to say something I'd regret, so I forced myself to put it in the form of a question rather than an accusation.

"I said, 'What happened to her anyway, Mr. Oliver? She looks as if she's had some sort of an accident that burned her.' He stood quickly and kicked the TV switch off, sending the stand rocking and almost tipping the whole set over. I was frozen in my chair.

"He swore again and said, 'How do you know what kinda sores she's got on her body? I never seen any sores on her.' Now I was livid. I said, 'Why don't you ask her mother or call her in here and see for yourself?' It was the first time I sensed any vulnerability in the man. He said, 'She fell down the stairs about a month ago and she burned herself on the hot plate about a week later.' "

"Did you believe him?"

"Would you have? Being burned on a hot plate is a mighty unusual injury, other than on a finger. Anyway, the Social Services doctor put in his report that many of the burns appeared to have been caused by cigarettes. I stood and moved toward the door. I thanked him for his time and left him with a not-so-veiled threat.

"I said, 'I'd hate to have to report to Social Services that this is an unsafe home for a little girl.' "

"He let you get away with saying that?"

"Not entirely. He said, 'You're gonna find out that this ain't a safe place for you.' And he started toward me. His wife cried out, and as I ran down the stairs I heard him laughing. By the time I reached the door on the first floor, he was screaming at her."

"I'm surprised he let Heather come to preschool after that," Jennifer said, "now that the cat was out of the bag. These guys usually protect themselves."

"She didn't come again for more than a month. I panicked. I asked her friends if she was still around, and they assured me she was. I walked

through the neighborhood several times, and occasionally I'd see her, but when she saw me, she'd run away. Finally I talked to Elliott."

"Really? You hadn't talked to him for quite a while by then."

"Right, but I ran into him at the park and asked him how he liked school. We probably talked more for those few minutes than we had all the time he'd been in preschool. It was so sweet. I asked him if there was anyone at school who sneaked him doughnuts and rolls, and he smiled so shyly and with such obvious gratefulness at the memory that it made my whole career here worthwhile."

Angela invited Jennifer into the building and into her tiny, cluttered office where she poured two cups of black coffee. "I have to admit," Jennifer said, "even after all you've told me, I don't feel like I know those two kids."

"That's just it," Angela said. "I never felt that way either. When kids don't express themselves, you tend to assume characteristics based on how they look, how cute they are, how shy they are. I'm sure I've got both Elliott and Heather idealized in my mind. To me, they were both precious children. Victimized. They had that look like you had, that look Oliver gives people."

"That look?"

"Like they've just seen the devil himself."

"He left you with that look twice, didn't he, Angela?"

"Three times."

"Three?"

"I saw him once more. This is the good part. I threatened him."

"Whoa, back up a little!"

"Well, Heather started coming to preschool again; and she appeared healthy. There were no signs of any injuries. She was running and playing and talking with the other kids. Things were fine for probably six months."

"That long?"

"I'm not saying she wasn't still being abused. I'm sure she was. But the man was being careful. I mean, he'd always been careful enough to keep from hurting her where it would show. But I noticed no tentativeness, no physical tenderness, and she finally even started talking to me."

"Really?"

"Nothing big. Just greetings and questions. Very shyly, very quietly. I tried desperately to build a relationship with her so she would tell me the next time she got hurt. That was a pipe dream, but I tried."

"And did she?"

"Tell me, you mean? No. I found out about the next incident through Nathalie at Social Services. They got a call from the emergency room at

St. Anthony's. The mother had brought Heather in during the middle of the night with an unbelievable injury."

Angela stopped talking. Jennifer waited. Angela straightened papers on her desk and stacked some books on the shelf. When she finally spoke again, her voice was thick. "Jennifer," she said, "if you want a crusade, a campaign, an issue, it's the red tape in this city! We're choking on it!"

Jennifer didn't understand, but she wasn't about to interrupt Angela now that her anger was boiling over. She had apparently been so crushed by the death of Heather Lauren that she had been unable to fully express it. If it was coming out this way, that was fine. It would be good for her.

"It's not Social Services' fault. They have no more power than the Park District does. All they can do is file reports and make recommendations. I think they should have recommended Heather and Elliott's removal from that home after the first physical exam, but they advised observation instead.

"But when they got the report from St. Anthony's, they moved quickly. As far as I know, the paperwork is still floating through city hall somewhere."

"Can you tell me about the injury?"

"The girl was nearly dead, Jennifer! They had to perform artificial resuscitation on her twice in the emergency room!"

"What had happened to her?"

"She was in shock. She could have died from the shock. Shock is probably what really killed her a few days ago."

"The autopsy will show that. But why was she in shock that first time?"

"Lots of bruises and burns, but a horrible injury to her seat." Again Angela was too upset to talk, but Jennifer wanted to hear it all.

"To her seat?"

"Oh, Jennifer," Angela whispered, "Nathalie showed me a picture that I can't erase from my mind." And she cried.

"I saw one of those recently too."

"You saw that picture?"

"I saw the one taken by the police in the cellar where she was found."

"I don't want to see that one. The emergency room photo was all I ever care to see."

"Can you tell me about it?"

Angela walked to the window and stared out across the parking lot. The sun was now hidden, and the day had turned gray. "The skin was burned black, and the only thing recognizable was the brand name of the hot plate, which had been seared into her in reverse. Someone had sat her on that hot plate!"

"What was the mother's story?"

"She just wanted them to hurry, because she said her husband, whom she listed as Wyatt Lauren, had forbidden her to bring the girl in, but he was sleeping and she needed to get treatment and hurry back. The hospital wanted to admit Heather, but her mother refused. That's when they called the police."

"The police were involved in this before? I didn't even know that."

"You didn't know that the West Side homicide sergeant wanted the kids out of there but couldn't get the clearance?"

"No, but I'll be asking him about that today. What did Mrs. Lauren tell the police?"

"Her story was that Heather had sleepwalked, fallen down the stairs, landed on the hot plate, and passed out from the pain or from hitting her head or something. They asked why her husband had not wanted her brought in for treatment, and she said he didn't have money or insurance and thought they could take care of her themselves."

"And the police believed her?"

"No. In fact, Wyatt Oliver was held overnight for questioning."

"I wonder why none of the media are aware of that," Jennifer said. "You're sure of this?"

"That's what Social Services told me when I screamed at them about getting the kids out of that house. They said they'd done everything they could think of. I could think of something else."

"Such as."

"If you can't separate the children from the parents, you have to separate the parents from the children."

"How do you do that?"

"When Wyatt Oliver was released and I realized the full import of what was going on—"

"Meaning?"

"Meaning that the man had apparently almost killed the girl and was now back in the same home situation. I stewed for a day, then walked through the neighborhood. Heather was outside, watching the other kids play. Elliott was very attentive to her, checking with her every few minutes.

"She was pale, cold, stiff. When she walked, she hardly bent her knees. It was pitiful. I stormed to her apartment building and charged up the stairs. I surprised the life out of Wyatt Oliver.

"I banged on the door so loudly that they didn't want to answer. I said, 'I know you're in there, you lazy bum. Answer the door!' His wife opened the door, and he stood behind her with a small stick in his hand.

"'You gonna use that on me?' I asked him, 'or do you only beat up little girls?' His wife hid her face in her hands and started to move away, and he acted like he was going to come at me. I wish he had. I'd have killed him."

"Do you really think you would have?"

"I know I would have. He's a strong guy, but I was so pumped up I could have torn him in two with my bare hands. He saw it in my eyes, Jennifer, because he was scared to come closer. I said, 'Come here, you slime,' and he tried to slam the door on me. I put my foot in it and took a good bruise to the ankle, but not before I promised to make him pay with his life."

"You really did?"

"You bet. I said, 'If one more thing happens to those kids, Oliver, I'll kill you.' "

Seven

"I'm glad, for your sake, that you didn't fulfill your promise, Angela."

"There's still time."

"Don't say that."

"I read your column, Jennifer. Don't tell me you and a lot of other people wouldn't love to do it for me."

"I wouldn't."

"Then your column was a lie?"

"I didn't say in my column that *I* wanted to mete justice out to the murderer."

"Oh, I see. You want him to die for the crime, but you wouldn't want *your* pretty hands soiled in the process."

"Angela, you're upset. You know what I mean, and I know what you mean. And I have to believe that you don't seriously intend to do harm to a person you can't even be sure is guilty."

"I'm sure. Are you saying you're not?"

"How could I know?"

"You know. Don't you know? You had an encounter with the murderer today, didn't you?"

"How could I know he was the murderer, Angela?"

"Will you get off this Pollyanna kick? You look into your heart of hearts and tell me you've got one shred of doubt whether that scoundrel murdered his own daughter."

Jennifer couldn't speak.

"One shred," Angela challenged again.

Jennifer stared at her.

"All right," Angela said, "so get off your high horse."

"But Angela, you're a mature adult. You know you can't throw your life and career away by actually killing a man."

"I know what you're saying, Jennifer, but I'm so tired of the bureaucracy, the stalling, the jive. Who needs this? Society lets this man get away with everything short of murder, and now it appears he's going to get away with *that!*"

"He won't get away with it."

"Not if I have anything to do with it, he won't."

"What would you do, Angela, if he really did slip through somehow? If through further investigation, they couldn't find enough evidence to convict him?"

Angela Liachi sat heavily across from Jennifer and looked deep into her eyes. "If it happened today?" she said. "If I learned it today and I saw him today and I had the opportunity, I fear I would kill the man. And I mean that."

"Do you want me to protect you from yourself?" Jennifer offered.

"What do you mean?"

"You want to take a few days off and cool down, come and stay with me for awhile? You sound serious."

"I *am* serious. You think I'd like that, don't you? You think I'd welcome the chance to get out of this rat hole, start thinking like a rational human being, and enjoy the comforts of your Uptown place."

"It isn't that."

"It isn't? Then what is it? You want me for column material? You promised not to write about my motivation for working here, but you didn't promise you wouldn't write about my motivation for murder. Am I gonna read about this in the paper tomorrow morning?"

"Of course not."

Apparently Angela believed her, because she finally broke down and sobbed. "I appreciate you," she admitted through her tears. "And I'm sorry I said that. I've known you only a little while, but I can tell you wouldn't use me."

"And the little I've known *you*," Jennifer said, "tells me you really don't want to end your career by committing a murder."

Angela's shoulders heaved. She shook her head. "I don't really," she said. "I'm like you; I want someone else to do it. It scares me though. I really think I'd do it if I saw the man today."

Jennifer stood and poured more coffee. Angela appeared surprised that Jennifer would feel free to do that. She thanked her and asked, "Want something on-the-record that even the cops don't know yet?"

Jennifer was almost too shocked to respond. "Are you serious?"

"Sure. Get out your pad. You remember Mrs. Lauren told the cops that Heather didn't come home from preschool? And that she didn't report her missing or tell anyone else outside the family until she found her in the basement two days later? Well, Heather hadn't been to preschool for weeks, and she definitely wasn't there Monday."

"I don't get it."

"Neither do I."

"The police didn't come asking?"

"No, and they should have, shouldn't they?"

"Of course."

"I'd been asking around about Heather. The kids said she was still in the neighborhood but that she couldn't come to preschool. I thought maybe she was being abused again, and I walked through the neighborhood a few times, but I always missed her. Either that or she avoided me."

"Likely?"

"Under threat of her father, if you can call him that? Sure."

"So you really hadn't seen her for a long time?"

"Not since right after she'd been treated for the hot plate burns."

"Why didn't you come forward when you saw the misinformation in the paper?"

"I just did," Angela said.

"And I can quote you on this?"

"That's what I said."

"Thanks for everything, Angela. And do me a favor, will you? Don't do anything rash, regardless of what happens with Wyatt Oliver."

Angela forced a smile, but said nothing.

Not a half hour later, Jennifer was waiting to see Nathalie Benedict at the West Side Social Services Center. The receptionist kept relaying questions from the inner office. "You won't need much time? You'll accept no-comment reactions when Mrs. Benedict feels they're necessary? She can be off-the-record when she requests it?"

Jennifer agreed to everything. Finally, she was ushered in. Nathalie Benedict was a tall, pleasant, healthy-looking, almost handsome woman—classy, but past her prime. In her mid-fifties, she still carried the evidence of an early season tan, aided by heavy makeup, coiffed hair, lots of jewelry, and expensive clothes. Her nails were long and painted lavender to go with her layered outfit.

"You're covering the Lauren case?" she asked.

"Yes, ma'am, thank you for seeing me. I wonder if you can tell me about the time you had Heather Lauren examined by a Social Services doctor."

Mrs. Benedict grew cold and stared at her. "When I what?"

"When you took a doctor into the West Side Park District preschool at the request of the teacher and staged a bogus class physical so the doctor could get a look at what Heather Lauren had told the teacher were 'ouchies.' "

Mrs. Benedict lit a cigarette and squinted as she took a deep drag and, instead of blowing the smoke away, merely opened her mouth and let it curl up in a thick column. "I have no comment about that," she said evenly.

"Are you saying it didn't happen?"

"I'm saying I prefer not to comment about it."

"Did you yourself see the injuries on Heather Lauren's body?"

"No," she said, and quickly realizing the implication of that added "comment."

"No? Or no comment?"

"No comment."

"Can you tell me about the injury to Heather Lauren that your office was made aware of several weeks ago when she was taken to St. Anthony's emergency room in the middle of the night with third-degree burns to the buttocks?"

"We were made aware of that, yes."

"And did you make a recommendation based on that?"

"Our recommendations to the police and other agencies are matters of public record."

"Then you won't mind telling me what that was?"

"Our recommendations? I don't remember. You may feel free to look it up at city hall."

"Did you not recommend that both Heather Lauren and her older brother, Elliott, be removed from their home?"

"I don't recall."

"Does it not sound logical?"

"Without studying the documents, I couldn't comment—"

"Are you saying there's a possibility that you didn't recommend that a child be removed from a home where such injuries had been inflicted?"

Mrs. Benedict had not appreciated being interrupted, and while it was not Jennifer's usual style, she sensed there wasn't a lot of time on this case. Wyatt Oliver either had to be indicted or exonerated, and she was beginning to share Angela Liachi's frustration over the red tape.

"I will talk with you off-the-record," Mrs. Benedict said suddenly, surprising Jennifer. "Do I have your word?"

"Yes, ma'am." But Nathalie didn't start talking until Jennifer returned her notebook to her purse.

"I know you have been talking to Miss Liachi, because you couldn't have known of the physicals otherwise. And I want you to know I share her anger and misery over this death. But I also want to make clear that I need my job, I want my job, and I have never made a practice of bad-mouthing my agency or the police or the courts."

"I understand. Is there something you would tell me off-the-record about them, however?"

"I must have your word."

"Absolutely confidential."

"My prediction is that this Oliver will never come to trial. They so seldom do. It was obvious from the way Cornelia Lauren acted that night in the emergency room that he had abused the child and also that the whole family was terrified of him. She would not budge from the crazy sleepwalking story, and she has never pressed charges against the man for any reason.

"Strange as it may seem, as many times as our agency has been in that home and been aware of the abuse, and as many times as Angela Liachi has taken it upon herself to do our work—and I don't blame her for a little zeal—the man has never been charged with one crime similar to what was committed this week."

"Nothing? No public disturbance, family quarrel, anything?"

"The only thing on his record, and the police will bear this out, is some public drunkenness. We have recommendations in, yes. I would like to see the kids, well, the boy now, removed from that environment. But someone had better get something on that quote/unquote father, or Elliott will grow up right where he is. If Oliver doesn't kill him, too."

"You know these people, don't you? I mean, you know their names as if you're familiar with the case."

Mrs. Benedict nodded. "All I can give you on-the-record is that we are aware of the case, we hope the guilty party will be found, and that our previous recommendations regarding the disposition of the family are on public record."

"That's it?"

"That's it. I wish I could be of more help."

"Off-the-record again, then. What are the answers for cases like this? What can anyone do to speed things along, to get action, to protect children from such an environment?"

"Besides killing the abusive parent you mean? I wish I knew."

"I wish you hadn't said that."

"You have been talking with my friend, Angela, haven't you?"

"Uh-huh."

"Don't worry about her. She blows off a lot of steam, and she's usually right on the money. But she's not going to do anything more to Wyatt Oliver than yell and scream at him like she did once."

"She's not serious about wanting to kill him?"

"Oh, she's serious enough. I just don't think she would or could if she wanted to. Anyway," she concluded with a weary sigh, "if she really wants to, she'd better take a number and get in line."

Eight

Jennifer had a few hard questions for Sergeant Martin Grom at the West Side Precinct station. But he wasn't there when she arrived. That surprised her. He knew she was coming.

As she waited in the lobby and idly read the plaques and citations and Police Youth league trophies, she smiled at the memory of her first encounter with the man the officers call The Lug.

Grom was a big redhead, about six feet three inches and broad in a soft sort of way that wasn't flabby, but was miles from being in shape. He walked with his elbows away from his body, swinging his arms like a robot. People tended to stay out of his way.

He was gruff and blunt, but he waxed fatherly in the presence of the opposite sex. Jennifer's Jim had always gotten a kick out of Martin, and he seemed to have a decent reputation in the department. He often brought his kids in on his days off. Couldn't stay away, but had to babysit. He had a bunch of 'em, but all were boys except his five-year-old.

"Your daughter's name again?" Jennifer asked when The Lug finally arrived and waved her into his cubicle.

"Jackie," he said, not beaming as usual. "We call her Red."

"Everyone in your family have a nickname?"

"No, she's the only one."

Jennifer smiled, assuming no one called Grom The Lug to his face. "I don't think I've ever seen you in uniform before, Martin. You still in homicide?"

"Oh, yeah. I wear it now and then. Special occasions and so forth."

"This is a special occasion?"

"Nah." But he didn't appear eager to elaborate.

"Martin, can I ask you some questions?"

"I figured that's why you were here, hon," he said. "Fire away, but let's make it fast."

That wasn't like him either. She studied him for a moment, but he wouldn't return her gaze. "Why didn't you tell me Heather Lauren had been burned before?"

"What're you talking about?"

47

"I'm talking about St. Anthony's, the middle of the night, third-degree burns with a hot plate, holding Oliver for questioning."

"Ah, that was Oliver, wasn't it?"

"Oh, I get it. You didn't remember till just now."

"That's right."

"That's ridiculous. A man of your ability, your concentration, your attention to detail?"

"So what? What do you want from me, Jenn? OK, we tried to book the guy the first time around—"

"But that wasn't the first time around, Martin. Social Services wanted you to look into the family when they discovered injuries on the girl's body in a physical exam."

"Oh, yeah? You're onto everything, huh? Well, did whoever tell you that also tell you what kinda heat Social Services got for that little sham or how the fur would have flown if we'd used that little bit of information on this Oliver creep?"

"What are you saying?"

"You tell me, Brenda Starr, you know so much."

"Martin, don't be mean with me."

"I'm sorry, Jenn, but this girl has been dead probably since Monday, discovered only yesterday, and already I'm getting pressure to arrest somebody."

"Pressure from whom?"

"Whaddya mean from whom? From downtown, from the papers, from everybody. From you."

"Did I say anything like that?"

"Come on, Jennifer! You sit here all but askin' me why I don't have Wyatt Oliver in the slam. You think I don't get your drift?"

"I wasn't driving at that, Martin."

"Then what were you driving at?"

"I just want to know why there has been so much activity on the man, admittedly with no convictions, but without the press knowing anything about it?"

"We don't have to tell you anything you don't ask."

"But you have in the past, and I've appreciated it."

"I haven't given you much."

"That's the most accurate thing you've said so far." He looked pained, but she plunged ahead. "Tell me what kind of trouble Social Services would have been in if you'd used the evidence they turned up in the class physicals."

Grom stood and rested an elbow on a bookshelf next to his desk. He sighed. "Awright, you can't give physicals without parental consent. All

we needed to do was use that information and it would have come out that they'd pulled a bogus deal. Other parents with kids in that class would've demanded to know if their children had been examined in that scheme, and then the whole city would have come down on our heads. The evidence would have been inadmissible."

"So you had to forget it, even when she turned up terribly burned at St. Anthony's several months later?"

"We put a lot of heat on the man, Jennifer. Hank Henry and I handled the interrogation, and I'd like to think we had the guy on the ropes. But the woman wouldn't point the finger at him. The little girl wasn't talking. The neighbors heard only screaming and crying and an argument about taking her to the hospital. Oliver didn't give Cornelia Lauren permission to take Heather to the hospital, so she had to wait until she could get him dead drunk, and she almost waited too long."

"That's not enough to focus on him?"

"It's nothing! The woman was there! Without her testimony, for all we know the kid could have fallen down the stairs onto the hot plate!"

"Martin! What would the hot plate be doing at the bottom of the stairs? And how could she have landed on it in a perfect sitting position and stayed there until she'd suffered third-degree burns and branded herself? And why would the hot plate be turned on in the middle of the night?"

"OK, Jennifer, the man is guilty, all right? I know it. You know it. Social Services knows it. Cornelia Lauren knows it. Heaven knows Heather knows it. And you can bet Elliott knows it too."

"Then why can't anything be done? I don't understand it."

"It's the system, Jenn."

"The system! Martin, this sounds like a B movie! Everyone's powerless to fight the system?"

"I tried! I offered to take those kids into my own home! You've got to have a smoking pistol, or the next best thing, in court. I go in there with circumstances and shouting in the night, and I'll come out with an acquittal. That's worse than no indictment in the first place. I'm trying to get the District Attorney to indict now, but we can't use Wyatt Oliver's history."

"Why not?"

"Because according to the law, if he wasn't convicted, it never happened."

"Let me change subjects here for a minute, Martin. How do you know Heather Lauren didn't return from preschool Monday?"

"You got our official statement. It came right off Mrs. Lauren's written statement."

"May I see that?"

"The written statement?"

"Yes."

"You promise not to quote directly from it?"

"Of course."

Sergeant Grom dug it out from a pile in the middle of his desk, leafed through it, and produced a photocopy of a thick, handwritten sheaf. Jennifer scanned it quickly until she came to the following:

I send Heather of to scool at 12.30. She dont com home at 2.30 lik everday. I wate and wate and send Elliott to lok.

"Did you check this out?" Jennifer asked.

"I assume someone corroborated it."

"Who?"

"I don't know. We have a lot of people on this, Jenn."

"Has anyone talked to her preschool classmates?"

"What do three- and four-year-olds know that can help us?"

"That she wasn't at school that day."

Grom stared at her, unblinking. "She never made it to school?"

"Did you talk with the preschool teacher?"

"I assume someone did."

"You're assuming too much, Martin. I talked with her, and no one from the police department has asked her anything."

"And she's saying the kid didn't make it to preschool that day?"

"She's saying Heather hadn't been coming for weeks. She didn't expect her that day."

"What's this woman's name?"

"Angela Liachi."

"I'll check it out. Liachi, you say?"

"Liachi."

"We've got something on her."

"Meaning what?"

"We got a complaint about her."

"From whom?"

"Are you ready for this? From Wyatt Oliver."

"You're serious?"

"Yeah. Just a minute. Hank!"

"Yeah!"

"Bring me that complaint Wyatt Oliver filed on the Liachi woman, will ya?"

Jennifer could hear grumbling from over the partitions as a pudgy, grimy detective brought in a manila folder. "In uniform today, huh Sarge?" he said.

Grom grunted and thanked him. He shuffled back out.

"Here it is," Grom said, sitting again and picking his way through the carbon paper. "Threatened my life," he read, "said she would kill me if she saw another bruise on one of my kids. I don't have to take that from anyone, blah, blah, blah."

"So what'd you do with it?"

"Sent somebody over to tell her that a threat on someone's life was illegal and that she could be charged with assault, not to mention battery, manslaughter, and/or murder if she ever followed through with her threats."

"She deny making them?"

"No. Told us if we wouldn't do our job relating to Wyatt Oliver, she would. We don't make a big deal of this type of a thing. We try to get the parties to talk and resolve their differences. In this case, it was apparent that that would not be the best approach, so we just let it drop."

"Is that why you never asked her to corroborate the mother's story? You were afraid she would do something drastic?"

Martin studied her. "You have a lot of insight," he said.

"And you guys are pretty naive. You think she wouldn't find out about the murder unless you told her?"

He was taken aback. "Are you turning on me, Jenn?"

"I'm not turning on you, Martin. But I'm saying you've got more than enough to lock up Wyatt Oliver."

"You gonna say that in the paper?"

"I don't know. Probably."

"That's gonna make us look bad, Jennifer."

"You do look bad, Martin."

"I've got to ask you not to do it."

"I can make no promises."

"It'll be the end of our friendship, Jennifer. It'll be the end of any information you get outta me."

"Do you think I care about any of that, Sergeant? I want to be objective. I want to play this straight. I don't want to be a crusader, and it's not my place to tell you what to do or how to do it. But I have to tell you, you've got a woman and a child living with a murderer who should have been locked up months ago. I don't know how you can sleep at night, Martin. I should think you'd have Heather Lauren's blood on your hands."

He stood quickly and glared down at her, and she knew she'd been too harsh. *Who do you think you are?* she asked herself. *One day with a column assignment and you start accusing cops of killing kids! She raised both hands to him.* "I went too far, Martin. I'm sorry—"

But he wasn't listening. His intercom had buzzed, and he pushed the lever to answer. "What is it?" he bellowed.

"A death, possible homicide, forty-three twenty-six West Stivers."

Jennifer gasped and stood as Grom came charging around the desk, pulling his dress blue coat off the hook. She found herself in his way, but only temporarily. He clubbed her just below the neck with the back of his hand on his way out and knocked her back into her chair without even looking at her.

Her elbow had banged the arm of the chair and throbbed. She caught her breath and jumped up to follow Grom, but as she neared the front door, he was already climbing into an idling squad car. She sprinted the half block to her car and gave chase, but she lost him and had to rely on her memory to get to the Oliver-Lauren residence.

She screeched to a stop a block away and found the 4300 block cordoned off by squad cars, paddy wagons, an ambulance, and several unmarked squad cars.

People were streaming from the surrounding buildings to as close to the scene as they could get. Jennifer joined them, wondering who Oliver had killed this time. As she neared the roped off area, she saw Elliott Lauren in the backseat of a squad car with a woman she assumed was Cornelia Lauren.

She detoured and asked the woman to roll down the window. "Are you Cornelia Lauren?" she asked the ashen face.

The woman nodded, but the officer at the wheel lurched around and shouted, "Hey! Get away! Roll up that window!"

"I'm with the press," Jennifer said.

"Get away!"

At least they were safe. She moved to the edge of the rope and started to crawl under. "You can't come in here, lady," a cop told her.

"I'm Press," she said.

"I don't care if you're the Queen of England," he said. "Nobody but police are allowed in here right now."

"What happened, Officer?"

"Somebody got snuffed, that's all I know."

"Did Wyatt Oliver do it?"

"I didn't hear any names. Clear the way!"

Evidence technicians were jogging up the walk, with cameras and black boxes at their sides. Jennifer knew that as soon as they had marked the spot where the body had been found, they'd release it, and the medics would carry it out.

"You really don't know if the perp has been apprehended or who was murdered?"

The cop shook his head and ignored her.

In a few minutes, plainclothes detectives escorted a middle-aged black man from the apartment building. He was not handcuffed, so apparently he would simply be questioned. He stared at Jennifer as they approached, and as they passed, he shouted:

"That's her! That's her! That's the chick I saw in the house the last time I saw Oliver alive!"

Nine

A detective with the black man told the uniformed policeman, "Don't let her out of your sight," and kept moving.

"Hey, Officer, uh—"

"Officer Huber, ma'am, please stay right here with me."

"Officer Huber, you don't have to worry about me. I'm Jennifer Grey with the *Chicago Day*. I was here earlier, yes, but on assignment. I saw Oliver, but—"

"So, who's Oliver? The dead man?"

"I assume, yes, but—"

"I know nothing about the case, lady. I just can't let you outta my sight."

"Well, listen, when people come out of that house, I may be moving up and down the line here asking them questions. Can I do that?"

He looked worried.

"I'll keep waving at you to let you know I'm still here," she said. "Fair enough?"

"I don't know."

"Here, take my wallet, better yet, take my car keys. I can't get far without these."

"Lady, I don't want any of your stuff. You just stay right here, 'cause I'm gonna hafta answer for you."

Martin Grom emerged from the building, leading another couple of cops and the paramedics, who wheeled a litter containing a covered body. The crowd edged forward. Jennifer felt strange, being the only media person on the scene. They'd be here soon enough, she decided.

"Who's the dead man, Sergeant?" she called.

"You know who he is, Jennifer," Grom growled.

"See, Officer Huber, I know the sergeant."

He just stared at her.

"Martin," she called, grabbing his arm and slowing him, "will you tell this guy I can be trusted?"

Grom was disgusted. "What's the trouble?" he asked.

"The black guy they're questioning says he saw her here before the murder," Huber explained. "Cap'n Halliday told me to keep an eye on her."

"I was here for a few minutes before going to see Angela Liachi, Martin," Jennifer said. "She can prove I wasn't here when Oliver was killed."

"Don't kid yourself, Jenn," Martin said. "Angela Liachi is our prime suspect."

Jennifer was speechless. *Of course*, she realized, *a person who had made a definite threat and was even named in a complaint would have to be the first suspect.* There had been a prerequisite to her threat—harm to one of the Lauren kids—and that had been fulfilled. Could Angela have been worked up to such a frenzy by their chat that she had actually followed through with her plans? Jennifer couldn't believe it.

"Then can I go?" she called after Grom.

"Just stay accessible, you hear?" he yelled back.

She nodded.

"It's all right, Huber!" Grom added. "We know where to find her."

Several other uniformed and plainclothes cops emerged from the building. "How'd he die?" Jennifer asked.

"No comment."

"Angela Liachi the only suspect?"

The men looked at each other and at her. "We have no suspects as yet."

"How'd he die?" she asked again, hoping someone in the back of the group had not heard the "no comment" from the front.

"Fork," someone said.

"Fork?"

"Fork to the back."

"Common kitchen utensil?"

"You got it."

"From his own house?"

"Can't tell yet."

"Fingerprints?"

"Don't know yet."

"Where was he found?"

"On the landing between the first and second floors."

"Happen there?"

"Probably outside his door on two."

"Thank you. May I go in?"

"Not till the evidence techs come out."

"His wife and child see the murder?"

"No comment."

"She a suspect?"

"No suspects yet."

Jennifer, as was her custom at such scenes, returned to her car and waited for the crowd to disperse. There wasn't much to see once the body had been removed, and people generally drifted away, just as the broadcast media rolled up to take long shots of the building.

After about twenty minutes, TV camera crews began setting up out front in the growing darkness, their lights illuminating street reporters in the front yard reading somber messages from cue cards, telling of the bizarre slaying of a man whose daughter had been found in this very building the day before, and whom many had considered a suspect in that death.

Jennifer walked around the block and came through the back alley to the side door. The cops supposed to be watching that door were ogling the TV reporters in the front yard. She took in the scene and casually walked through the open door and up the steps, careful to touch nothing.

Evidence technicians were crouched everywhere, dusting for prints and tracks, taking blood samples from the stairs. They basically ignored her except to direct her around the areas where they worked.

She began to realize the idiocy of walking through the scene of a crime in which she herself was a suspect, but she was more overcome with the sense of evil in this place. She'd been at murder scenes before. But never this soon after the event.

She believed Satan was the author of death, the robber of life, and when a murder motivated by anger or hatred was perpetrated with such horrible violence, it carried the stench of evil. A feeling of fear and dread was almost physical in the place.

She prayed silently as she mounted the stairs. *Lord, protect me, cleanse me, be with me.*

The door to the Oliver-Lauren apartment was open, and the lights were off. "Have you been in there yet?" she asked the technicians.

"No, ma'am. Not yet."

She hurried back down the steps and out the door, drawing a surprised look from Officer Huber, who was now stationed at the side of the building. "Good evening, Officer," she said. He nodded.

Jennifer couldn't make it all compute. Why would the apartment door be open and the lights off? If Cornelia Lauren had been the perpetrator, wouldn't she have done it while he slept? Had she been there when it happened? If so, she would have either seen or had a good idea who had murdered Wyatt Oliver.

Had Elliott been home? Was he capable of such an act? She doubted it. Surely he could have had a motive if he had been treated as his sister had. But he was so small, and Oliver was so strong. Maybe, if he had surprised the man—but with a fork? Unlikely. The fork pointed to Cornelia. But what was that Jennifer had seen in the backseat of the squad car? A bag of groceries? Had she been out and discovered him when she returned? Who would know?

Jennifer went back out into the alley and to the other side of the building next door. She rapped on the door and jumped back as a black face appeared immediately at the window. *Of course,* she realized, *everyone's been watching everything.*

"Excuse me," she said, "but could I ask you a few questions?"

"Depends on who you are," said a male voice.

"I'm Jennifer Grey of the *Chicago Day.* "

"If I talk to you, I might be in the paper?"

"You might be, unless you don't want to be."

"I do. Come on in."

Jennifer hesitated, knowing immediately that her hesitation would probably offend the man. She walked in slowly and up a short flight of stairs to a tiny kitchen. The man, who looked to be in his early twenties, was long and lanky and wore a new white T-shirt and blue jeans with no belt. He was barefoot.

"Chair?" he said, pointing to a vinyl covered, aluminum framed one.

"Thank you."

"Coffee?"

"Thank you."

He scowled as if he'd wished she'd said no, and moved toward the stove.

"Oh, if it's any trouble—" she said.

"No trouble," he said, unconvincingly.

"You don't mind talking to me and being quoted in the paper?"

"Are you kidding?" he said. "Might be the highlight of my life."

She smiled. "Name?"

"Lionel Whalum," and he spelled it for her.

"Age?"

"Twenty-five."

"Occupation?"

"None."

"You live here alone?"

"Nobody lives in this neighborhood alone," he said, sitting across from her and waiting for the coffee to perk.

"Family?"

"I live here with my mother and her brother. We're the only people on this block without kids."

"Can you tell me what you saw today?"

"Everything."

"Meaning?"

"I saw you earlier today."

"You did? You did see everything then, didn't you?"

"Yes, ma'am."

"What else did you see?"

"You mean around the time Oliver bought it?"

"Uh-huh."

"Kids were playing all over the place. Elliott was with them."

"How far from his apartment?"

"Down the block."

"Where was Mrs. Lauren?"

"His old lady? She was out with somebody from Social Services."

"How do you know that?"

"I saw the car. Someone from the agency comes every now and then and takes her shopping, showing her how to get more food for less money and food stamps, that kinda stuff. They do the same for us."

"And then they brought her back when?"

"They didn't bring her back. She walked home."

"Is that normal?"

"Yeah. Store's not that far away. They come for you because they know you probably wouldn't show otherwise. But they don't have to take you home too."

"Does this happen on some kind of a schedule?"

"Yeah, but nobody knows what it is 'cept Social Services. They just call and say they're coming to take you to the store, and it's usually within a few days after you get your check and your food stamps."

"Uh-huh. Did you see who it was from Social Services?"

"No, I just saw Cornelia get in the car."

"Did Elliott go along?"

"No, he went back into the house for awhile. Then he came back out to play."

"What else did you see today, Lionel?"

"I saw another reporter. At least, I think he was a reporter."

"What did he look like?"

"Big, tall. Young. Dark hair. Big glasses. Wore boots. Walked around the front of that building and took a lot of notes. I don't know if he actually went in or not, 'cause from where I am I can only see the front and the sidewalk and the back alley, I can't actually see the side door."

"Was this guy wearing a denim suit?"

"Right. You know him?"

"I think so." She sure did. It sounded like Bobby Block. *What would he have been doing there? Maybe murdering Wyatt Oliver and trying to make it look like I did it? Good grief Jennifer, you're paranoid. The kid is a scoundrel, but he wouldn't go that far to get your job!*

"What did you see me do today?"

"I knew you went inside because I saw you go around the side and heard you holler at Elliott. And then you didn't turn up in the back alley or come back out the front until you came running. I figured you must've met up with Oliver in there. I was hoping you'd killed him, but I saw him in the backyard about a half hour later."

"You'll swear to that?"

"Sure."

"And he was healthy?"

"Yeah!"

"And the other reporter came when?"

"While Mrs. Lauren was gone."

"You see anybody else?"

"I saw the preschool teacher."

"Angela Liachi?"

"Uh-huh." He poured the coffee.

"When was this?"

"I saw her two or three times. Mid-afternoon, before Mrs. Lauren left. Then while she was gone."

"Did she go into the building?"

"I don't think so. I saw her in front and in back, but never at the side."

"What was she doing?"

"Just talking with the kids and watching them and roaming. Just like always."

"How do you know her, Mr. Whalum?"

"We know everybody who comes through here. It's safer that way."

"I suppose it is."

"For everybody 'cept Wyatt Oliver anyway. We don't do much to protect that man."

"Apparently not."

"Can you blame us?"

"Do you think he killed Heather?"

"Everybody knows that. He's been beatin' on those kids since they moved in here."

"Who found him today?"

"She did."

"She?"

"His old lady, Cornelia. She came back from the store with a bag of groceries, waved 'hi' to Elliott, and the next thing I know she's out front of the building screaming to call the police, call the police."

"Did you call?"

"Me? No. I got enough trouble with the police. I don't need that. Anyway, there's enough people in her building to call. They never go anywhere."

"There didn't seem to be anyone there when I was there."

"They don't come to the door unless they know you. And they wouldn't have called the police for him."

"I thought you said they would."

"They would for her. Not for him. If it was him yelling to call the police, they'd have just shut the doors. They like her. She's good people."

"So then what happened?"

"Elliott came running to his mama, and she liked to tackle him to keep him outta that building. She set the grocery bag down and grabbed him in both arms and held on for all she was worth until the cops got here. That's when I knew Oliver musta bought it and was lyin' in there somewhere. 'Course, news travels fast, so soon enough I got the story."

"What is the story?"

"People in my building think someone in his building got him with his own silverware. This gonna be in the paper?"

Ten

"I've just been sitting here reading, wondering when I would hear from you," Jim said when Jennifer called.

"I assume you've heard what's going on," she said.

"Yeah. You need an ear?"

"I sure do, love. But it might be kinda late. I've got two pieces to write tonight, and I have to talk my way out of being a suspect in this thing myself."

"That I hadn't heard!"

"I saw Wyatt Oliver before he was murdered, and I was seen. But I'm not worried about that. I'll tell you all about it later. Can I call you and meet you somewhere?"

"Sure."

"How late?"

"You name it. I'm off tomorrow, remember?"

"Oh, that's right! Thanks, sweetheart. I'll call you as soon as I can."

Jennifer had broken a boot heel in the alley behind the Oliver apartment building, so while she was in the phone booth, she decided to let Leo know she would be stopping by her apartment on the way in.

"You know the cops are looking for you?" he asked.

"Yeah. Who called?"

"The redhead from the West Side. Is it serious?"

"Leo, for now I'm a suspect."

"Tell me you're kidding."

"I'm not. But I've also got a witness who saw me at the Oliver place and who also saw a healthy Wyatt Oliver after I left. And I was with Angela Liachi and then Nathalie Benedict and then Sergeant Grom the rest of the afternoon."

"The cops are placing the time of death at late in the afternoon, Jennifer. Were you en route somewhere around that time?"

"Sure, I could have been going to or from any one of those appointments. I was with Grom when the report came in."

"Did you go back to Oliver's late in the afternoon?"

"Not until after he was dead. That's where I'm calling from now."

"Give me the details on your eyewitness, and I'll try to get you cleared through Grom. That'll give you time to run home on your way in if you want to, and I should at least be able to get you enough time to do your two pieces before they send you to Sing Sing."

"Not funny, Leo."

"Sorry. But don't dawdle."

Jennifer knew the doorman at her building would keep an eye on her car, so she parked in front instead of in the underground garage and limped in the front door, gobbling a fast-food burger on the way.

"Your sister is waiting for you, ma'am," the doorman said.

"My sister?"

"Yes, ma'am."

"Thank you," she said, looking warily into the lobby. From an overstuffed chair in the corner, peeking aver the top of a magazine, were the fearful eyes of Angela Liachi. "Angela!" Jennifer said, a little too loudly.

"Hi, Sis!" Angela said, making a show of embracing her. Then she whispered, "I've got to talk to you!"

Jennifer took her upstairs while she changed into low-heeled shoes and freshened up. "So, what are you doing here?" she asked, pointing Angela to the couch.

"I decided to take you up on your offer to get me out of that rat hole so I could cool off for a few days."

"Angela!" Jennifer said, emerging from the bathroom. "You know the police are looking for you?"

"I know. I did a very foolish thing, Jennifer." Her voice grew husky and her eyes filled.

"Oh, please—" Jennifer said, dreading what she was about to hear.

"I shouldn't have even walked over there."

"Angela, if you're about to make a confession, I—"

"It was a dumb thing to do," Angela continued in a monotone, ignoring Jennifer and staring past her. "I was in a mood after I talked to you. I thought about you sitting there with Nathalie Benedict and then going to see that homicide guy, and I knew you'd find out that they couldn't use the evidence they found by giving those phony physicals. "

"Angela, please, if, if, I don't even want to know right now if—"

"—and I knew that nothing would be done, because nothing ever gets done about people like Wyatt Oliver." She began to cry.

Jennifer stood over her with her hands on Angela's shoulders. "What are you going to do, Angela?"

"I want to stay here for awhile. May I?"

"I have to get into the office to write my stories. Is one of them supposed to say that I'm harboring the murderer of Wyatt Oliver?"

"I didn't say that, Jennifer! I wanted to kill him, but I couldn't bring myself to go inside! I hate myself because I didn't do it, but I'm sure glad it got done."

Jennifer flinched. She had suppressed the same reaction to the murder, knowing all the while that it was a horrible thought. To be glad that a man has been plunged into eternity, and knowing that he certainly met a godless end—

"So you didn't do it."

"No. Nathalie told me after my first episode with him, when I threatened him, that I would never really be able to do it."

"You discussed it with her?"

"Sure. She said she thought she could do it if she felt as strongly about Oliver as I did, but she didn't think I could."

"Dangerous talk."

"I know. But, Jennifer, you haven't worked with the low-lifes in this city the way we have. You haven't faced the system. You haven't seen innocent people suffer and guilty people go free because of delays, continuances, payoffs, deals, bargains, neglect, and incompetence."

"Do you think Nathalie Benedict could have murdered Wyatt Oliver?"

Angela buried her face in her hands. "I don't know," she said. "I really don't."

Jennifer looked at her watch. "I need a commitment from you, Angela."

"Hmm?"

"I need you to look me in the eye and tell me you didn't see Wyatt Oliver today."

"I didn't."

"I want to believe you."

"You can."

"Based on what you're telling me, I'm going to take the risk of harboring you for a few hours."

"Harboring me?"

"You're wanted by the police, Angela, and I know it. That means I'm protecting you from them. But let me tell you this: If they ask, I'll have to tell them the truth."

"Could you call me and let me know if they're coming?"

"No, I couldn't do that. I shouldn't even do this, but if I give you to them, they'll detain me as well, and I've got work to do first."

"What do you want me to do?"

"Just stay here. Don't answer the door, and don't answer the phone unless it rings seventeen times. If it does, that's me."

"Thanks, Jennifer."

"Don't be too quick to thank me. We both may regret this soon enough. I've got to call Leo. That reminds me. Don't use the phone."

"I won't."

Jennifer dialed. "Leo, I'm leaving right now."

"I'm surprised to hear from you, Jennifer. Grom says they're staking out the parking garage in your building right now."

"Luckily, I parked in front, but I'd better hurry or they'll tow me away. They may be waiting down there for me now, or on their way up."

"I don't like it, Jenn, and neither does Cooper."

"Cooper knows about this?"

"He's got contacts everywhere. What are you going to do?"

"I'll do whatever you say, Leo."

"You sure you can clear yourself in this deal?"

"Of course."

"Grom says the eyewitness you quote is a known pimp."

"Terrific, Leo. If I'm going to try to get there without them seeing me, I've got to go right now. If you want me to just turn myself in, I will."

"Come on in. Let's see if you can get the stories done before we have to give you up."

Jennifer ran to the door, pointed back at Angela and said, "Remember what I told you. Just stay put. I may not be back until morning."

"What?" Angela said, but Jennifer was gone, sprinting past the elevators—she was sure the police were on their way up—and down the far stairway. She ran down nine flights of stairs, fearing at every turn that she would see cops who were supposed to be in the basement garage.

When she reached street level, she peered around the exit door a half block south to the front windows where the doorman was pointing two uniformed policemen to the elevators. Apparently they had not seen her car yet or were convinced that she was upstairs. She ran to her car and drove to the office.

Cooper and Stanton and Bobby Block were waiting for her when she got off the elevator at the far end of the city room. "Follow me," Leo said, and they headed for a small office that formerly housed the news wires and now was used for paper storage. A video display terminal had been plugged in.

"We're going to stall them for as long as we can," Cooper said, "but as soon as your stories are written, we're going to turn you over to them."

"You're going to stand by me, aren't you?"

"Of course we are," the big boss said. "If you say you're innocent, you're innocent. But we can't hide someone who's wanted by the police, and we won't. At least, not for long."

"I have a question for Bobby," Jennifer said.

Bobby squinted at her. Leo and Cooper looked at him.

"Any reason you can't do the straight story?" she asked.

He shrugged.

"What's she talking about, Block?" Leo said.

"How should I know? Ask her."

"Watch your mouth, kid. You're talking to your boss's boss in front of his boss," Max Cooper said, showing a remarkable familiarity with the hierarchy.

"Well, I don't know what she's talkin' about!" Bobby whined.

"Why were you at the scene of the murder today, Bobby?" she asked.

"Who says I was?"

"I do."

"Are you saying you weren't?" Leo said.

"Well, no—"

"Then why were you? You weren't assigned!"

"Well, somebody has to handle the police beat while Susie Columnist here is posturing for the publisher!"

Everyone fell silent, but Max Cooper was hot. His forehead and ears reddened. Finally, he said, "Leo, I don't want to see this person anymore. Get rid of 'im."

Leo and Bobby headed down the hall, leaving old man Cooper with Jennifer for a moment. "Write me a good column, huh?" he said. "Leave out anything about you bein' a suspect; we'll deal with that. The straight piece oughta write itself. Put your energy into the column, 'cause it's your column that's gonna make this paper over the next few years."

He winked at her and left, and while she was flattered by his confidence, she hadn't decided to accept his long-term column offer, and she could have as easily burst into tears and begged for twelve solid hours' sleep as try to write.

Besides not knowing what to think about the fact that her salvation from being a suspect was in the hands of a known pimp, she wanted to see Jim and talk to him about all the dangling clues in the case.

Neither did she know yet whether Angela Liachi had been straight with her. For all Jennifer knew, Angela *had* murdered Wyatt Oliver. Jennifer's conscience was already nagging her for protecting Angela from the police, guilty or not. The same was true of her own flight from Sergeant Grom.

For a minute she toyed with insisting that Cooper and Leo turn her in, but at the same time she was nudging the elements of her column around in her head. As they fell into place, she began writing:

I'm facing difficult emotions as I compose these words. The man most people assume murdered four-year-old Heather Lauren has himself been murdered, not a full day after I championed capital punishment for whoever had done it.

And so now what am I supposed to think? How am I supposed to react? How are you reacting? Cornelia Lauren may now feel free to tell what really happened in that home, fearing no reprisal from her common-law husband.

It won't surprise anyone to learn that Wyatt Oliver tortured the girl, let her go too long without eating, intimidated her mother to the point that she couldn't even protect her own daughter, went too far with his methods, and wound up killing Heather.

We'll find that he carried her to the basement of the apartment building in the middle of the night, probably Monday, and tied the lifeless body to a post, for there are no signs of struggle or blood in that basement now, and he attempted to make it look as if she had been abducted.

We'll find that she died from shock, but that any of several injuries inflicted on that vulnerable, defenseless little frame could have done her in. And then we'll be glad that the perpetrator got his.

Or will we? When we know for sure it was Wyatt Oliver, will we still be glad he's dead? You see my dilemma? If he murdered Heather Lauren, I'm glad justice was done. But the justice was not carried out in a just way.

There was no trial. So, unless Cornelia Lauren, one of two people in the world with firsthand knowledge of the first slaying, committed this murder, the perpetrator was making assumptions. And evidence will surface to clear Mrs. Lauren.

I spent time today with several people who are so frustrated with the "system" in this city, the bureaucracy that favors the guilty and harms the innocent, that any one of them could have had a motive to murder Wyatt Oliver. By the time I finished talking with them, I shared their feelings.

I saw Wyatt Oliver alive today. I left him with no shadow of a doubt that he had killed his own daughter. It's a strange feeling to see a man a few hours before he meets a violent death.

And I wrestle with the emotion that tells me that as one who believes in the sovereignty of God, one who believes that vengeance is His, one who believes that God is the author of life and that Satan is the author of death, I should not have any positive feeling whatsoever related to the death of a child abuser. I'll keep praying about it; and I don't say that flippantly.

Eleven

Jennifer was in the middle of rapping out the straight update article on the entire case when Leo knocked at the door.

"They're here," he said. "We've admitted you're here, and we've promised that you'll go with them if we can just let you finish your story. If you need it for the piece, Mrs. Lauren has been cleared, and she has named Oliver as Heather's murderer."

Jennifer was surprised half an hour later when she entered the city room and was arrested by Martin Grom himself. As he was quietly reading her her rights, Max Cooper caught her eye from behind the sergeant and pointed to Gerald Mayfield, the newspaper's counsel.

Jennifer was flabbergasted that they would have thought to call him and ask him to represent her. "I have counsel," she said. "Thank you."

Grom was surprised too. Mayfield introduced himself "This isn't so magnanimous as it seems, Mrs. Grey." Mayfield said. "I happened to be in the Loop tonight anyway."

"Still, I'm grateful."

"Don't mention it. Sergeant, may my client and I have a few minutes?"

"Well, I gotta tell you, Counselor, my partner is waiting in the car, and the people here have been harboring this woman for quite some time—"

"Martin, you told me earlier that it was OK and that you knew where to find me," Jennifer said.

"Yeah, but when we looked at your place, all we found was Angela Liachi. We'll have to bust you for harboring her, at least."

"Well," Mayfield said, "which is it? Are you arresting her on suspicion of murder or for harboring a suspect?"

"We haven't decided yet."

"Then while you're thinking about it, surely you wouldn't mind if my client and I spent a few minutes in private."

Grom shrugged, grimacing.

Jennifer and the dapper Mayfield wended their way through clusters of desks and tables to the far end of the huge city room, finally sitting across from each other on a desk top. "I'm so sorry about this," Jennifer said. "It's

all my fault, and I know I shouldn't have gone to the Oliver place today, and—"

"Just hold on a minute, Mrs. Grey. The worst thing you've done so far is to let this Liachi woman stay in your place. If she's guilty, that'll compound matters."

"She isn't."

"You can't know that."

"I'm pretty sure."

"Well, I should hope so."

"There's something strange going on here, Mr. Mayfield. Sergeant Grom said his partner was waiting in the car. Does it make sense that the numbers one and two men from West Side Homicide would be here looking for me? It seems anyone could come and round me up."

"True enough. So what are you saying?"

"I'm worried about Martin."

"Martin?"

"Grom, the sergeant. He's been very distraught since we spoke today. This case is really getting to him."

"That uniformed sergeant is the Homicide Chief on the West Side?"

"Yes."

"And his assistant would be whom?"

"Hank Henry."

"And Grom works for whom?"

"Captain Halliday, I believe, Chief of Investigative Operations."

"You have the number for the West Side Precinct?"

Jennifer recited it to him.

"Good evening. Gerald Mayfield of Bransfield, Mayfield, and Beckman calling for Captain Halliday, please . . . John? Gerry Mayfield here. How you doing? . . . Good! Me too. Listen, do you have a minute? . . . Yeah, I know. I'm involved in it too now. I'm representing the *Day* and their reporter Jennifer Grey . . . Yes, she's been arrested actually. John, can you tell me who's heading up this investigation for you? . . . Oh, you are. Well, what about your Homicide Chief over there, Sergeant, uh . . . right, Grom. What's he doing? . . . Excuse me just a minute, John.

"Jennifer, Halliday tells me he's given Grom the rest of the night off. Says he's taken control of the operation himself."

She raised her eyebrows.

"John, the man is here right now. He's handling the arrest of Mrs. Grey himself. Is that what you want, or can I bring her over to you myself? . . . Sure, hang on."

Mayfield hurried over to Martin Grom and told him he was wanted on the phone. After a few minutes of intense conversation with his boss, Grom stormed out of the city room. Mayfield took the phone again.

"What's his problem, John? . . . Ah, I see. Five-year-old, huh? Good man though, right? . . . Sure. We'll be over. Thanks, John."

Jennifer was puzzled.

"Let's go," Mayfield said. "We can talk in the car. I want you to tell me all about your day."

"Happy to," Jennifer said, following him out, "but what's happening with Grom?"

"Well, seems he's a father himself. Bunch of boys and a five-year-old daughter."

"I know."

"That's why he's taking this case so personally. He's been working on it around the clock. It's been affecting him."

"In what way?"

"Halliday says Grom wore his uniform today because he thought it was the day of the monthly meeting of the Fraternal Order of Police. But that's tomorrow."

"An easy mistake."

"Not for Grom. He's secretary of the Chicago chapter."

"What pushed Halliday into sending Grom home?" Jennifer asked as they approached Mayfield's car.

Mayfield stood at the open door as she got in. "When Grom and Henry brought the Liachi woman in, she told Halliday she'd never been questioned about Heather Lauren, even though Mrs. Lauren said she never came home from preschool."

"And?"

"Halliday was upset. To him, that was a major omission by a homicide sergeant, and he thought it was time Grom got some rest. They're all getting a lot of heat from downtown, and somebody is holding Halliday himself responsible for getting the thing cleared up."

"Am I going to be spending the night in the lockup, Mr. Mayfield? If I am, I need to call my boyfriend."

"I think you'll be able to see your boyfriend tonight, Jennifer. I'll try to have you out of there on your own recognizance—or mine as soon as possible. John Halliday and I are old buddies."

Jennifer tried to give Gerald Mayfield every detail of her day, recreating much of it from her notes. He was not happy about her having entered the crime scene before the evidence technicians were finished.

"You know they have fantastic equipment," he said. "They'll find some trace of you there."

"Well, as I said, I had been there earlier in the day, too. And the evidence men saw me there, so there won't be any hiding that."

"I don't want to hide it. But if you hadn't been there at all, and there was therefore no trace that you had been there, they'd be hard pressed to try to say you had anything to do with Oliver's murder. You were there before and after, so who's to say you weren't there during?"

"You are."

Mayfield laughed. "True enough. But you've made my job a bit more difficult than it needed to have been."

"I'm sorry."

"Nonsense. I enjoy the challenge. You are innocent, aren't you?"

"Pardon me?"

"You are innocent, are you not? You didn't murder Wyatt Oliver, did you?"

"What do you think?"

"I think I'd better coach you on how to answer a direct question. I am not kidding when I ask you that, and neither will John Halliday be kidding. And you can be sure he will ask you. People will be asking you that, and every time you are asked, you would serve yourself well by looking the interrogator in the eye and telling him the truth."

"Even if I'm guilty?"

"Even more so. You'll notice that I didn't tell you what to say; I just said to tell the truth."

"I didn't murder Wyatt Oliver, Mr. Mayfield."

"Thank you. That was encouraging. Do you know who did?"

"No, sir."

"Very good. Do you have an idea who did?"

"I have fears."

"Care to speculate?"

"I don't know. There are so many people who wanted to. Myself included."

"It would be good if no one else in an official capacity heard you say that."

"But it's the truth."

"Fine, but if you are innocent and want others to believe you, you'll keep quiet about your own motive, means, and opportunity. You see, the fact that you were at the scene before and after means that you had the opportunity. Everybody in town had a motive, it seems. The means? Well, someone who was in that apartment got to the table or silverware drawer in time to use a fork on Oliver, probably to make it look as if his wife did it."

"I worry about Nathalie Benedict and Angela."

"So do I. Using a fork could be construed as a feminine means of attack."

"But I'm talking about the timing," Jennifer said. "It had to be someone who had access to the schedule of when Social Services was taking Mrs. Lauren shopping."

"A good point," Mayfield said. "I'm surprised too that Oliver would let his wife out of the house, since she was the one person who knew that he had murdered Heather."

"He probably had her convinced that she was as much at fault and that if he got in trouble for it, she would too."

"Yeah, but mother-love usually transcends things like that," he said, "especially after the daughter is gone."

"Who knows?" Jennifer said. "Maybe she was getting ready to spill the beans."

"Have you ruled out the son?"

"Elliott? Too small."

"Means, motive, opportunity," Mayfield reminded her.

"I don't think so."

"Neither do I, but don't overlook anyone. Including your eyewitness."

"My eyewitness? The pimp? How much help is he going to be?"

"His record and his occupation have little to do with his credibility."

"They should, Mr. Mayfield. That's another problem with the system."

"For now, don't knock it. He may be the only one who can clear you."

Twelve

As Gerald Mayfield and Jennifer entered the West Side Precinct station house, Jennifer caught sight of Jim waiting in the lobby. She ran to him.

"I heard about it on the radio," he said.

"Heard about what?"

"Bobby got fired."

"Yes, and—?"

"And he's gone to the news media saying that you're the prime suspect, that you went crazy with all the publicity today's column brought you, and you acted out your fantasy of capital punishment on the murderer of the child."

Jennifer was speechless. Jim held her.

"I suppose this bearer of good news is Jim," Mayfield muttered.

"Yes, I'm sorry," Jennifer said, making the introductions.

"Nice to meet you, Mr. Purcell. So what else did Bobby say?"

"He said another suspect was found in Jennifer's apartment and that there is speculation about conspiracy. Sounds crazy."

"It is crazy," Mayfield said. "We'd better go in, Jennifer. You'll probably have to wait, Purcell."

Before ushering Mayfield and Jennifer into Captain Halliday's office at the back of the building, the desk sergeant told Mayfield he had a message to call Leo Stanton at the *Day*. The conversation was brief, but after Mayfield hung up, he said, "We'll be initiating litigation against your former assistant, of course."

"Of course," Jennifer said.

Captain Halliday in many ways reminded Jennifer of an older Sergeant Grom. He didn't have the same mannerisms, and was in fact almost grandfatherly, but he was a large, rangy man. His white hair was thinning, and his full face was rosy, eyes sparkly.

He didn't rise when they entered but rather sat back and sized them up over the tops of his half glasses while pointing to chairs. Mayfield detoured to shake Halliday's hand first.

"Good to see you again, Gerry. And Jennifer, we've met. And I've worked with your intended a time or two."

"Oh really? Well, he's not really my intended, but—"

"Whatever, let's talk about why my crack homicide boys think you might have murdered this child killer, not that I wouldn't have wanted to do it myself."

"You know, John, that's what everybody's been saying all day," Mayfield jumped in. "People who read Mrs. Grey's column this morning, and even people who didn't. It seems she can't run into anyone who doesn't share that sentiment."

"Is that so? Well, I guess nobody loves somebody who could do something like that, do they? But nonetheless, we can't go around taking the law into our own hands, now can we?"

"Of course not," Mayfield said, "but—"

"Gerry, I'm gonna have to ask you to let Mrs. Grey here speak for herself."

"Well, John, I appreciate that, but I am her counsel, and I prefer to represent her."

"I don't mind, Mr. Mayfield," Jennifer said.

"Yeah," Halliday said, "and any way, this isn't anything official. I just want to have an off-the-record chat. I won't hold anything you say against you in a court of law, as we have to say these days, an' you don't quote me in the paper, fair enough?"

"Sure!"

"Uh, can we stipulate something here, John?" Mayfield said. "I need to feel very comfortable here, as you're trying to make us feel, I think—"

Halliday winked at Jennifer, "These lawyers are never comfortable unless they're stipulatin' something, are they? All right, Gerry, just what is it you want stipulated?"

"I want to clarify that this is not an official interrogation and that nothing my client says here can or will be used against her in court."

Halliday swore and then excused himself to Jennifer. "Isn't that what I just said, Gerry? We go back a long way. You know me. I said I wanted to clear this up. I don't want any trouble with the media, and I don't want to detain this young lady any more than we have to. I said I wouldn't use anything against her, but I'll sure listen to everything that might clear her without further trouble. It's late, Gerry, and I'm sure we all want to go home. Don't you?"

"Yes, but—"

"Well, then just take me at my word like you've always known you could. All right, I know it's out of the ordinary for a cap'n to talk to a suspect off-the-record after she's been read her rights; do I hafta admit that

Grom was way out of line to be bustin' somebody after I tol' him to go home? OK, let's get on with this, and I'm stipulatin' whatever it is you said, which I had already said. Let's work on getting this over with so I don't have to deal with a false arrest charge and you don't have to worry about court."

"I'll stipulate this," Mayfield said. "If we leave here tonight with no charges pending, there'll be no false arrest claim. And I haven't even cleared that with my client."

"OK with me," Jennifer said.

"Good," Halliday said. "Can we finally begin?"

They both nodded, smiling.

"I must tell you," the old man began, "that even though my little homicide crew is distraught and overworked and has made its share of errors here lately, they don't lightly arrest someone on suspicion of murder. As I understand it, you have been placed at the scene of the crime."

Jennifer nodded and started to speak. But Halliday continued.

"I'm also aware that one of the neighbors says he saw Oliver after you were there, and that he was healthy."

"Yes, when I came running out of there the first time, it could have looked like I had done something wrong."

"Well, it did. Do you have any idea how many people saw a well-dressed woman run from that building and speed away in her car? The next thing they know, it's several hours later and Oliver is dead. If this, uh, Whalum, Lionel Whalum, hadn't seen Oliver about mid-afternoon, you'd be in big trouble."

"I'm glad you talked to him, because I was relieved when he told me—"

"Yes, I'm aware that you also talked to him. That was not a wise thing to do."

"Why?"

"If you were aware of the man's profession, you wouldn't have wanted to be alone with him."

"I'm aware now."

"You saw his Cadillac with the multi-colored headlamps and the fur-lined rear window?"

"No. Was it there?"

"It usually is."

Hank Henry brought in some documents for the captain. "Did you get him home all right?" Halliday asked.

"Yes, sir," Henry whispered. "I'm sorry, sir, but I hadn't been apprised of the fact that he had been ordered off duty until he told me at the *Day* offices."

"That's all right. I know how intent he is on solving this one." He glanced at his watch. "You got here fast. He still lives on the Near North Side, doesn't he?"

"Yes, sir, but he just had me drop him off at the Chevy dealer up here on Lester. He'd dropped his van off there this morning."

"Surely they're not open this late, are they Hank?"

"No, sir. But he had extra keys, and they always let him settle up later."

"It's after midnight, Hank. You goin' home?"

"Yes, sir, but I'd kinda like to see this thing wrapped up too, and I thought maybe if you had time, I could run a few of my thoughts by you."

"If you want to hang around, Hank, I'll be here. But if you head home, I'll understand."

"I'll be here."

"Dedicated man," Halliday said. "You deal with him much, Jennifer?"

She shook her head. Halliday leafed through the papers Hank Henry had delivered. He read, half aloud and half to himself, so Mayfield and Jennifer caught only bits and pieces:

> Blood on stairs not an hour old when technicians arrived. Door casing to Oliver apartment had been shattered, apparently by a kick just under the doorknob. Lab tests show partial rubber print of sole and heel indicate possible oversized men's shoe, approximately thirteen, extra wide, possible quad E, brand Apache Workmate.

"Good shoe. My dad wore 'em in the factory. Used to use 'em on the street when he walked the beats in the fifties. Not really regulation, but they were comfortable. Never wore out."

> Door had knocked out jamb and swung all the way to wall, where knob drove hole into wall. Signs of struggle in the kitchen, silverware drawer open, blood on kitchen table, living room rug, wall near door, second floor landing, copious amounts on stairs and banister, body found on landing between first and second floor.
>
> Coroner is estimating that the pound strength required to drive common kitchen fork through the latissimus dorsi muscle and to break a rib and puncture the heart would

indicate that the perpetrator was either unusually strong or extremely agitated.

Halliday looked up. "Well, that kinda goes without saying, doesn't it? Somebody kicks Oliver's door in, beats him to the silverware drawer, starts poking him in the back in the kitchen, and chases him down a flight of stairs. I'd say whoever it was was agitated, wouldn't you?"

He didn't wait for an answer.

> Coroner has determined eleven distinct puncture wounds, two to the deltoid muscle, seven to the latissimus, and two to the fleshy area in the lower right back. Assuming the victim was running away, the perpetrator was either significantly taller or inflicted all the wounds from a higher step on the stairs—unlikely because of the blood trail. Three of the puncture wounds affected the heart, and it's likely that the fatal blow was not the final wound, whatever that means.

"I suppose it means the murderer could have left after fewer stabs," Mayfield said. Jennifer felt sick.

"You don't look tall enough or strong enough or agitated enough to have done this, Mrs. Grey," Captain Halliday said. "Did you murder the man?"

She looked him straight in the eye. "No, sir, I did not."

"May we go?" Mayfield asked.

"Not just yet. Let me see what else we've got here. Ah, interviews with neighbors in the building."

> No love lost. Heard the door breaking, assumed it was Oliver himself. He's done it enough times. Heard the scuffling, thought he might be punishing the boy again. Heard feet running on the stairs and the tumbling to the landing. Heard male screaming, probably Oliver. Heard heavy footsteps running out. Saw no one.

"Yeah, I'll bet," Halliday said, then he continued.

> Called cops? No. They never come for disturbances with Oliver anymore. Frankly, wishing he would get it one of these days. Figured maybe the wife did it, but when she screamed for cops, it was several minutes later.

Halliday peeked over his glasses again and looked at Jennifer, then at Mayfield. "The man's lucky his wife showed up. The neighbors probably would've just walked over him for a few weeks. This frankly makes me wonder if someone in the building didn't do it. Maybe a bunch of them did it, just like that murder on the Orient Express."

Halliday turned back to the report.

> What did neighbors notice unusual that day? Woman nosing around at about noon, running away within the half hour.

"That's you, huh?"

> Preschool teacher wandering through as usual, at least twice during the mid-afternoon.

"We've got her locked up in the back. Lot more points to her than you, frankly, but she doesn't look any too tall or strong either."

> Tall young man in western wear looking around, early afternoon.

"That one's worth checking out."

Jennifer caught Mayfield's eye, but said nothing.

> Mrs. Lauren went shopping in Social Services vehicle. Not unusual, except driver appeared to be the director herself, Mrs. Benedict.

"Don't know what to make of that. No one says she was in the building at all."

> Neighbors in the building and next door noticed police traffic at Whalum residence, approximately 4:00 P.M.

"Wonder what this is?"

> Kids in neighborhood corroborate this, and one also says he saw gray panel truck type vehicle pull into back alley. But no one else saw this, nor did youth see it pull away. Also unemployed men talking at corner saw unmarked squad car at Whalum residence for approximately twenty minutes.

Halliday looked agitated. "Hank! You still here?"

There was no response. Halliday grabbed his phone and dialed the desk. "Yeah, is Hank Henry out there? Tell 'im I wanna see 'im!"

Henry came chugging back and was surprised to see that Jennifer and Mayfield were still there.

"Sir?"

"These your notes?"

"Yes, sir."

"Well, what'sis all about, police activity at Whalum's around four o'clock? You tellin' me there were cops there that close to the time of the murder and we didn't hear or see anything?"

"At the time I wrote that, sir, I was unaware of the time similarity. Apparently I could have been in the neighborhood not long before the attack."

"You?"

"Yes sir, it was me."

"What were you doing at Whalum's, Hank?"

"Just putting a little heat on him, sir. Sergeant Grom, who used to deal with him a lot when he was in the Vice Control Division, got a call from VCD recently complaining that Whalum was apparently plying his trade unchecked on North Avenue and West Division. They were running the girls off, but they couldn't get to Whalum."

"So what was your assignment, Hank?"

"Grom asked if I would just pay him a call, mostly for looks. Let people see the unmarked squad in front of his place, embarrass him a little, that type of thing. I just talked with him for a while, told him the heat was on and that no one up here accepted any bribes or anything like that."

"Sounds pretty small time when we're on a much more important case, Hank."

"Yes, sir."

"But that's not your problem. I'll take it up with Grom."

"Frankly, sir, I didn't mind doing it. Sergeant Grom has had a lot on his mind, and with his daughter and all, he doesn't cater too much to, um, pimps, sir. He didn't want to handle it himself, and yet he didn't want to let down his friends in VCD."

"I understand." Halliday smiled. "Sometimes it is kinda fun just to intimidate one of these bad guys, you know what I mean? Well, uh, Hank, what else did you get from the neighbors inside Oliver's building?"

"Not much. The one black guy, the one who saw Mrs. Grey here, he was very helpful. He's the one who called when Mrs. Lauren started screaming."

"When does he say he saw Mrs. Grey?"

"Between twelve and one, just like everyone else."

"Any other witnesses say they saw Oliver alive after that?"

"Yes, sir. At least three, including Whalum. And some kids. The kids all know him. Scared of him. Hate him."

"Ha!" Halliday said. "Wonder if the kids did it?"

The captain stood and stretched, and Jennifer realized how tall the man was. He looked suddenly older and more tired than when they first came in. "You've got enough witnesses that say they saw Oliver alive after you went runnin' away, young lady. That's good enough for me. Now I gotta ask you not to use anything you heard in here tonight in the paper. OK?"

"That won't be easy," she said. "It was most interesting."

"But we have a deal, don't we? Your lawyer even stipulated it, remember?"

Thirteen

Jennifer had dark circles under her eyes and was dragging on her way out to the lobby, but she was alert enough to ask Gerald Mayfield for one more favor.

"Sure, what is it?"

"Could you get them to release Angela? From what he just read, she doesn't have any more strength or whatever than I do."

"I'll try, but it'll be tougher with her. She could have been agitated enough, and she is on record as having threatened the man."

"Can we at least bail her out?"

"I'll check."

It took another forty-five minutes, and Mayfield had to post a personal bond—"based solely on your word, Jennifer; I don't know this woman"— but Angela was released. Jim offered to take her home and Jennifer back to her car at the *Day* office. Mayfield was grateful. "I can't thank you enough, Mr. Mayfield," Jennifer said.

"It was fun," he said, heading for his car.

"Did I get you in a lot of trouble, Jennifer?" Angela asked in the car.

"Some. Not much. Most of it was my own doing. They're going to waive the harboring charge. How are you doing?"

"Well, that wasn't my favorite way to spend a late evening. I was almost asleep. I wouldn't have bet a penny I'd be bailed out tonight. Good experience, though. Just taught me more about the crazy system."

"We keep coming back to that, don't we?" Jennifer said.

"Yeah," Angela said, but she was preoccupied, staring out the window.

Jennifer let her be for a few minutes, then asked what she was thinking.

"I'm a little scared, that's all."

"You wanna stay with me tonight?"

"No, thanks, not that kind of scared. Scared of me."

Jennifer wanted to pump her, but she was too tired, and she figured Angela was too, so she probably wouldn't elicit much. She was wrong.

"My reaction to this whole thing bothers me a lot," Angela began suddenly. "I've gone through moments when I wondered if I actually had

murdered Wyatt Oliver. I rehearsed it so many times. Not with a fork, of course, but whatever was handy."

She fell silent again, and Jennifer wondered aloud if there was anyone within blocks of where Wyatt Oliver lived who didn't have a motive to kill him.

"Probably not," Angela decided.

"And the one with the best motive of all didn't do it," Jim offered.

"Cornelia Lauren?" Angela said. "Don't be too sure. She's pretty shrewd in her limited way. She could have been planning this for a long time."

"But this soon after her daughter's murder?"

"What better time?"

Jim waited on the street until Angela was safely inside her building. "I'd love to hear every last detail," he said as he pulled away, "and I'm sure you're dying to tell me, hon, but you'd better save it."

Jennifer lay her head on his shoulder, turned sideways in the seat, and slipped both her hands under his arm. "Jus' wake me when we get to the office," she slurred. "I gotta talk to Leo for a minute."

"He'll still be there?"

She nodded. "He's putting the first section to bed."

In the *Day* parking lot a half hour later, Jim gently pulled his arm from her grasp and wrapped it around her shoulders. "Sweetheart," he said quietly.

"Um-hum," she said, eyes still closed.

"We're here."

She opened her eyes without moving. "So we are," she said. "I'm comfortable. How' bout you?"

He chuckled. "Why don't you just let me drop you at your place, Jenn? You can talk to Leo tomorrow."

"No," she said, sitting up. "It can't wait. What time is it?"

"Almost two o'clock."

"Ouch. What time does the sun come up tomorrow morning?"

"You mean this morning? I don't know—about seven."

"I'll check."

And with that she dashed into the building and up to see Leo. "Hey, hey!" Leo said. "How's my little fugitive?"

"Bushed. I gotta talk to you."

"Coffee?"

"Why not? It's too late to keep me up."

He sent someone for two cups. "So, talk to me."

"You remember the agreement I made with you and Mr. Cooper about Jim and me and police reporting?"

"Yeah, you haven't violated that, have you?"

"No. But I *would* like to know what you would do about the police beat if I left."

"If you left!"

"I mean, if I left the police beat, not the paper. With Bobby gone—"

"He's gone all right. I shoulda dumped him when he tried to get you in trouble the first time."

"Tried?"

"So, anyway, what would I do with the police beat if you left? Frankly, I'd have my pick of the news staff."

"You would?"

"Yeah. I told Cooper I thought you'd take the column."

"You did?"

"Uh-huh, and he suggested Bobby, but that was before this evening. After that, he said he would clear anyone I wanted, if they wanted to come."

"Got anybody in mind?"

"A few, yeah."

"Yeah? Are you to the point where you'll be disappointed if I stay?"

"I'll still be in charge of you, Jennifer, so I don't care what you do."

"You do too!"

"You're tight. I want you to take this column. Your piece tonight was—"

"How badly do you want me to take it?"

"As badly as Cooper does."

"Is that badly enough that you two slave drivers will rescind our little agreement about Jim and me?"

"You set me up, you turkey!"

She laughed.

"I don't know," he said.

"Come on, it's not the police beat. There'd be no conflict of interest."

"But your stories would often overlap with police stories."

"Like now."

"Right. What would you do then?"

"I'd use him."

"You'd use Jim?"

"You bet I would."

"And if we back off about you and Jim, you'll take the column?"

"I don't know yet. I haven't prayed about it or talked to Jim about it yet."

"Will you?"

"I won't even consider it unless that agreement is eliminated."

"If I told you it was eliminated right now, when would I get your answer about the column?"

"Soon. Do you have the power to rescind it?"

"Are you kidding? You ever see Cooper cross the Lion?"

They both laughed. "Forget the agreement," he added.

"You mean it?"

He nodded.

"Thanks, Leo!"

"The competition will be good."

"What do you mean?"

"C'mere, Jennifer. Let me give you a sneak preview of Jake Rogers's column, which will always appear opposite yours."

Jennifer read Jake's column off the film that would make up the front page of the morning's paper. He played critic, evaluating her work as a police beat writer ("gushy, gee-whiz reporting"), her two personal columns ("amateurish, sensational, emotional, religious"), and even the placement of the column ("call it professional jealousy if you will, but it took me six years of paying my dues before my column was placed on the front page").

"I'm shocked."

"Don't be. It's vintage Jake. And it's probably more entertainment than substance. I can't imagine he really feels that way, but he knows it'll sell papers."

"I have to tell you, I would never even acknowledge in print that kind of criticism."

"Of course you wouldn't, Jenn. If he keeps this up, we'll find out what the grassroots reader really wants."

"I don't want to take the column to prove something to Jake. I hardly know the man, and I usually enjoy his stuff, especially the humor. This doesn't humor me. But it does convince me that we're long overdue for an old-fashioned, conservative viewpoint."

"You know we are, Jennifer. Let me know soon, will you?"

"Leo, there's a method to my madness here, and I don't want to get thrown off the track by Jake Rogers's venom. Even if I don't take the column, I want you to rescind the agreement I made about Jim and me immediately, for the sake of tomorrow's column."

"You been working with him on something?"

"Of course not. I've lived up to my end of the bargain. But I'm about to ask him to help me with something. It may be crazy, but if it works, it could be a dynamite column. How 'bout it?"

"All right. But for tomorrow you're still writing two pieces, right? The straight one and the column."

"Right."

"And my pledge to you is that if you'll give me just forty-eight hours' notice when you're going to take the column assignment, you'll be off the police beat immediately."

"Thanks, Leo."

Jim was dozing in the idling car and jumped when Jennifer opened the passenger side door. "I'm sorry, Jim." He smiled and drove toward her apartment building. "You have plans tomorrow?" she asked.

"Just sleeping in."

"Can I spoil 'em?"

"You're the one thing I'd even give up sleeping in for. How's that for a sentence, Mrs. Hemingway?"

"It got the point across. I have a plan for tomorrow morning, before sunrise."

He groaned.

"C'mon," she said. "You'll still get four hours or so of sleep. And it'll be fun. You still have your evidence kit from cadet training school?"

" 'Course. Cost me more'n a hundred bucks."

"Got all the stuff?"

"Think so."

"You're gonna need it."

"You gonna get me in trouble?"

"No, unless there's something wrong with going over a crime scene after the evidence techs have already been there."

He thought a minute, parking in front of her building. "I guess not. What else can you tell me?"

"Dress warm. And be praying with me about my leaving the police beat and becoming a full-time columnist."

"I will. I'll miss you."

"Are you kidding? You'll see more of me than ever."

"Apparently so. Are we going to be too tired for dinner tomorrow night?"

"Highly unlikely," she said. And she kissed him good night.

Fourteen

It was cold in her apartment when Jennifer arose not four hours later. She liked to sleep with the window open slightly, even in the dead of winter. It made for good sleeping, but she paid dearly for it every morning on cold floors.

As she padded around the apartment in her bulky robe and slippers, she fought to keep her eyes open. Her breathing was deep and even, as if she were still in bed. But as she splashed cold water on her face and cranked up the coffeepot, her mind was racing.

She was convinced she would never get her eyes fully open and would probably look bedraggled to Jim, but she was still high with excitement. She'd had things rattling around in her brain ever since the conversation the night before with Captain John Halliday. She quickly ran down in her mind the list of things she had to accomplish to get out the front door by six; then she put herself on automatic pilot so they would get done even while she was thinking and praying.

One of the things she looked forward to in her future with Jim was the opportunity to spend time reading Scripture and praying with him everyday. She'd been doing it by herself for so long that she found she enjoyed it immensely when they shared it. Both were early risers by nature, so it would become a scheduled part of their morning routine.

She chastised herself for planning for married life with Jim when he hadn't even popped the question yet. But it was a foregone conclusion. They'd done a lot of talking about their future life together, but nothing close to a proposal had been made. That suited her. It had taken her a long time to get used to the idea of marrying again. In fact, for a long time it had kept her from even admitting to herself her deep feelings for Jim. But now she couldn't imagine a future without him.

Prayer was on her mind this morning too. She found herself thinking of the many people she'd been so intensely involved with the day before. Was it possible she had known Angela Liachi only one day? And Nathalie Benedict? She'd worked with Martin Grom before, but she'd never seen him near the edge like yesterday. Even Lionel Whalum came to mind, a

man so removed from her life-style that she didn't know where to begin to pray for him.

How should she pray for such people? Not one of them, as far as she knew, was a churchgoer, though some had indicated a certain God-consciousness. She guessed that that was where she should start, praying that God would somehow impress Himself upon them, get them thinking, make them receptive.

And then she prayed for opportunities to talk with them. She didn't know if she'd ever even see Lionel Whalum again, but she would undoubtedly see Martin Grom. And she could make it a point to see Mrs. Benedict and Angela. She knew she had something they needed, and she knew God could give her the words that could draw them to Himself.

Angela seemed especially sensitive, just by her nature and personality and by what she had been going through for the past several months. But someone else was tugging at the recesses of Jennifer's mind, and when she stopped for a minute and forced it to the surface, she knew immediately. Bobby Block.

There was no doubt he had gotten what he deserved. And it was probably the best thing that had ever happened to him. Not only had he been crushed by being fired, but when his ridiculous claims and conclusions about Jennifer were proved false, which would likely happen this very day, he would look like a fool.

She prayed that God would give her the resources to not retaliate. To show Bobby either by her silence or by the right word, should their paths cross, that she bore no grudges, that she wished him no further humiliation.

She knew if she could somehow glue together the loose ends in her mind this morning and if everything came together to support her wild hunches, she would not only play a major role in solving this latest development in the Heather Lauren-Wyatt Oliver murders, but she could also clear away all suspicion about herself.

She hoped that whatever happened would provide opportunities for her to interact with the principals of the case on a less emotional and rushed basis. *And I hope Jim is praying about this column decision,* she thought, *because I don't even have the time to think about it.*

Except that down deep she wanted to graduate to that job more than anything she had wanted in a long time. *I'll have to remind Jim to pray for my humility,* she decided. *Getting this thing out of perspective or thinking it's something I deserve can be dangerous.*

She snapped on her watch. Only a few minutes to spare. One last look in the mirror on her way to the front closet showed her furry boots, corduroy

Levis, a couple of layers of blouses and sweaters, topped by a cardigan buttoned all the way to the neck. She added a wool stocking cap and a down filled ski jacket and pulled on her mittens on the elevator after pushing the buttons.

She nodded and smiled to the doorman, who sat at his station looking as if he were ready for bed. He looked surprised to see her again so soon, but he didn't ask any questions. The morning was even colder than Jennifer expected, shocking her fully awake as she swung out the door, notepads tucked under her arm.

"How can you look so good so early in the morning after such a short night?" Jim said as she slid into the car. "I'm dead."

"Ah, we're both dead," she said, "but you don't look so bad yourself." Except for the colors, they were dressed nearly alike.

"Where we goin', Nancy Drew?" he asked.

"Head toward West Stivers," she said. "I'll be reading to you as we go."

"It won't take long, this time of the morning," he said. "Read fast."

She did. She sped through both notepads, reading everything she'd written, commenting on most of it, and adding tidbits here and there from memory. Then she recounted the entire conversation she and Gerry Mayfield had had with Captain Halliday the night before, including all the exchanges between Halliday and Hank Henry.

"How can you remember all that, Jennifer?"

"I work on it. It's fun. I've always been able to do it. The only thing I regret about last night is that I agreed not to use any of the Halliday stuff in the paper. Would make great copy, don't you think?"

"Yeah. Now what do you want me to think about it? Much of it was new to me; some of it wasn't. I heard a few interesting things, but for the sake of time—that is if there's something you want to do before the sun comes up—you'd better coach me a little."

"Well, what is it you've always told me about investigative work? Haven't you said it's the little things that slip past the first time, the seemingly insignificant things, the apparently unrelated things that wind up making the difference?"

"Yeah. It's always amazing how the things you hear somehow fit together. Later they make sense and you wonder how you almost missed them, but most people do anyway. Did you hear something that you think no one else picked up on? That's the type of thing that'll break this case."

"I tried to recite the stuff to you straight, Jim, without any inflection to give away what I think is significant. Did you pick up on anything?"

"Not really, but then I'm not really awake yet."

So she went back and selectively read and recited various elements to see if he agreed they fit together. By his movement and tone of voice, she could tell he was warming to her speculations.

"First," she said, "settle in your mind who might have had access to the schedule on which Social Services takes people shopping. The murderer had to know that."

"Right, OK."

"Then consider this: Angela Liachi may have been a viable suspect early on because of her threat, which had been on record. And she had been seen in the neighborhood, as I had. But neither of us were really solid suspects after the evidence technicians finished their work and after West Side homicide detectives had talked to the neighbors."

"True enough. So?"

"Well, after the autopsy, when the angle of the puncture wounds and the strength needed to inflict wounds to that back muscle and rib cage was determined, we were both in the clear."

"Right, and after the evidence technicians determined the shoe size of the foot that kicked open Oliver's door, I gotta think Halliday and Grom and Henry are looking for a big man."

"Yeah, but they may be looking too far."

"I don't follow you, Jenn."

"Don't you think Angela and I were scapegoats for awhile?"

"You maybe; she was a solid suspect for long enough. And scapegoats for whom? You think they have a more solid suspect they're hiding?"

"Or protecting."

"Hiding, I could see. Then they can reveal him at a press conference and take a lot of credit. Why would they protect a solid suspect?"

"Tell me this, Jim: why would Grom have arrested me at the office when his partner, Hank Henry, had already interviewed neighbors, three of whom said they had seen Oliver alive after they had seen me run from his building?"

"You said Henry was in the car when Grom was in your office, so he had to have told Grom."

"Sure he told him. Grom ignored it for some reason."

"Maybe he thought you knew too much, or he wanted to punish you for harboring Angela, whom he thought was the real murderer."

Jim approached the Oliver apartment building on West Stivers. "Pull around the side, Jim, but not in the alley. When I was in the alley last night, after being inside the building, I noticed only one place wide enough for a panel truck to fit. The driver could have pulled in and backed out, but he or she could not have driven all the way through the alley."

"Jenn, that gray, panel truck type vehicle business came from one kid. No one else saw it come or go."

"And what did you just tell me about little, insignificant pieces of evidence?"

"But does your whole case rest on whether that type of vehicle was in the alley?"

"Sort of."

"So that's why you wanted the evidence kit? For tire tracks?"

"Uh-huh."

"No guarantees in this weather. The ground could have been so hard that no tracks were left; of course, a vehicle that big might leave tracks anyway. But if the ground has thawed and refrozen since it was here—if it was here—we'll get nothing."

Jim pulled the heavy case from the trunk, and he and Jennifer dropped to all fours with a flashlight and crawled into the alley from the north. Almost immediately Jim held up a hand to stop her. "Wide tracks," he whispered. "You were right. There's no proof it's the same vehicle, but there couldn't be too many trucks that go back here. A garbage truck couldn't even fit in here. Hey, I can see the evidence technicians have been here."

"Yeah," Jennifer said, "but they don't know where to start looking for tires to match the tracks."

"And you do?"

"Of course, Jim. You think I'd get up this early otherwise?"

In minutes, Jim had mixed a special plastic epoxy and poured ten-inch squares on three different patches of good tracks. He also poured some in a shoe heel track. "I got a C in fingerprinting," he said. "But I was real good on tire tracks in frozen ground!"

He waited five minutes, then carefully peeled up the reverse images, which had the consistency of rubber. He also measured the distance between the tracks. As they headed back to the car, he said, "Anything else?"

"Nope. Not unless you want to look for the tracks of a woman who broke a boot heel back here, a little farther south in the alley."

"It wouldn't be hard to find. Now where do we go?"

"First, Jim, tell me how difficult it would be for anyone in either Oliver's or Whalum's building to see a vehicle parked where you made the track impressions."

He crept past a wood wall behind a ramshackle garage. "You're right," he said. "I doubt you could see it from there even if you were watching for it."

"But no one was watching for it."

"How do you know that?"

"Because everyone except one kid was distracted by police activity in front of the Whalum residence. Hank Henry was there twenty minutes, giving Lionel a little heat, remember?"

"Yeah. What are you saying?"

"You'll see. Take me about three blocks north of the West Side Precinct station, and I'll keep track of how long it takes us. Just drive the speed limit."

Fifteen

Less than ten minutes later, Jim pulled up to the curb across from the Chevy dealer on North Lester Avenue. The sun was rising, and employees of the service department were pulling into the lot.

When the big garage door opened, Jim drove in. "You're a little early," a young mechanic said. "What can we do for you?"

"I need to talk to whoever worked on Sergeant Grom's van yesterday."

"Is that the cop's, the big silver and gray job with the one-way windows?"

"That's the one."

"Melvin!"

"Yeah!"

"Guy's got a question here about the cop's van!"

Melvin, who was already greasy with the day hardly begun, jogged over. "Who's askin?"

"I am," Jim said.

"You a friend of Grom's?"

"Yes."

"Was there a problem? All we did was an oil change and lube job."

"No problem. He's gonna settle up today, huh?"

"I guess."

"Can I see the ticket? I'll be seeing him this morning, and I can tell him how much."

"Sure. I'll give you his copy. He's good for it."

The invoice showed that Grom had delivered the van a few minutes before eight o'clock in the morning, the previous day.

"He musta picked it up last night after closing, 'cause it was still here when I left."

"When was the work done?"

"Oh, let's see. I finished his by noon."

"You sure?"

"Yeah. Finished a Trans Am first, then Sarge's work comes next, every time."

"I'm sure he appreciates it."

92

"I hope so."

Captain John Halliday did not appreciate being awakened by Jennifer Grey after such a short night. But when he heard what she and Jim had uncovered, he agreed to meet them at the West Side station. He arrived less than a half hour later—unshaven, wearing work clothes under a red and black woolen hunting jacket, and having just dragged a comb through his white hair. "This is terrible," he kept saying, "but let's not jump to any conclusions."

When presented with all of Jennifer's reasoning, he propped both elbows up on his desk and held his head in his hands. He buzzed the desk. "What have you got for Grom yesterday between three-thirty and four-thirty?"

"Just a minute, Cap. Ah, yeah, away from the office on foot. Coffee break."

"Get Hank Henry on the line for me, will ya? Thanks."

Jim and Jennifer sat silently, occasionally catching one another's eye, as Halliday slumped in his chair. The intercom crackled. "Hank Henry on line two, Cap."

Halliday grabbed the phone. "Hank, I need you in here right away. Something's breakin' on the Oliver murder....I'll tell ya when you get here."

Jennifer started to speak as they waited for Henry to arrive, but Jim put a finger to his lips. Halliday wandered up and down the halls, reading messages he himself had posted on the walls, some of them years before, but which he probably hadn't noticed since.

When Hank Henry arrived, they all piled into Halliday's unmarked squad car for the drive to the Near North Side. Henry alternately nodded in recognition of the conclusions that were being drawn and shook his head at the realization that his boss was in terrible trouble.

At the modest home of Sergeant Martin Grom, the four stood on the porch and rang the bell. They could hear kids running through the living room and up and down the stairs. The TV was blaring.

The five-year-old girl answered the door. "Hi, Jackie," Jennifer said, eliciting a smile.

"Hi, Red," Halliday said. "Your daddy home?"

She ran to get him as her mother came to the door with a worried look. "Good morning, John," she said. "Is something wrong? Marty's still in bed."

"Just want to talk with him for a few minutes, Roberta. Can you get him?"

She turned to head up the stairs, but Martin was already coming down in a robe and slippers. He looked as if he hadn't slept. "Throw a coat on, Martin," Halliday suggested. "Wanna talk to you out here a minute."

Grom reached for a heavy parka from a hook by the door and pulled it on as he came out. "Let's take a little walk," Halliday suggested.

"I don't wanna walk around the neighborhood in my nightclothes, Captain."

"We aren't going far, Martin."

Mrs. Grom shut the door slowly as the unusual fivesome walked awkwardly down the front walk to the sidewalk, west a few dozen feet and back up the driveway toward the garage. Hank Henry looked as if he wished he could be anywhere else.

"Why did you arrest Mrs. Grey last night when you knew Henry had interviewed several neighbors who saw Oliver alive after she left him?"

Grom looked first at Hank, then at Halliday. "I had my reasons."

"I want to hear one."

"She was harboring another suspect."

"The other suspect wasn't much better, Martin. Why did you send Hank to see Whalum yesterday?"

"We often hassle these known baddies, Cap'n. You know that."

"Not in the middle of a murder investigation we don't. You sure you didn't send him as a decoy, something for the neighbors to watch while you did some business in the neighborhood yourself?"

Grom stood with his shoulders hunched and his hands deep in his pockets, the icy wind whipping at his pajama legs and bare ankles. His breath began to come in short gusts from his nose, his lips were pressed tight. He said nothing.

"You changed your clothes somewhere on the way to and from Oliver's place yesterday, didn't you, Martin?" Halliday pressed.

Grom couldn't hold his boss's gaze and looked at the ground. He began to tremble. Halliday continued.

"Our guys were supposed to be out this morning looking for a big guy, big feet, probably a blue-collar worker, maybe an old truck driving associate of Oliver's, somebody that mighta pulled a gray panel truck type of a vehicle into the alley behind his place."

Grom took his hands from his pockets and covered his face. "But the tracks from that alley aren't gonna fit some panel truck somewhere, are they Martin? We can call off our guys, the ones who would have been reporting to you today, can't we?"

Grom began to weep.

"You wanna open the garage door for us, Martin, and let us measure the wheelbase and compare the track molds and maybe look around in there

for a big pair of bloody shoes, maybe some gloves, maybe some work clothes?"

Grom shook his head.

"We don't have to do that, Martin? You gonna save us the trouble? You wanna admit that you wore your uniform yesterday so people on Stivers wouldn't recognize you as the same guy who'd come through the backyard in the middle of the afternoon? And that you borrowed your own van from the Chevy lot during your coffee break so it would look like it had been at the garage all day?"

Grom nodded, sobbing, as his wife emerged from the back door to embrace him. He nearly collapsed in her arms. "If only that Lauren woman had told me the truth on Wednesday!" he wailed. "If only she'd said then that he had murdered the girl, this wouldn't have been necessary!"

"You'll have to get dressed and come with us, Martin," Halliday said sadly.

"He was going to get off scot-free!" Grom moaned. "I couldn't let that happen!"

Epilogue

Today I write a column I'd rather not write. In fact it's a column I will never want to remember, but shall never be able to forget.

Today I saw a man's life and career disintegrate, a man who had given himself in service for his community and his family for years. Two days ago he told me, "If I had it my way, I'd kill Wyatt Oliver right now," and then begged me not to quote him. I didn't, but it no longer matters.

Yesterday he had it his own way, and today he confessed to the slaying of a child killer. A father himself, Chicago Police West Side Homicide Detective Sergeant Martin Grom will face the penalty for taking the law into his own hands, for giving up on the system, for plotting and carrying out his own form of justice....